I0631410

James Webb Rogers

Madame Surratt

James Webb Rogers

Madame Surratt

ISBN/EAN: 9783337334987

Printed in Europe, USA, Canada, Australia, Japan

Cover: Foto ©Andreas Hilbeck / pixelio.de

More available books at **www.hansebooks.com**

MADAME SURRATT;

A

DRAMA IN FIVE ACTS

BY

J. W. ROGERS,

OF THE WASHINGTON BAR.

———· ◄●► ·———

TO THE PUBLIC:

Harmony being now restored, and the Union preserved, I have endeavored to present the terrific scenes, with which our great Rebellion closed; and beg leave to suggest that the harsh expressions, put here into the mouths of both Confederate and Federal actors, find no place in my own heart, nor in the hearts, I trust, of any of my countrymen, in either section of the Union; but in writing a drama of the times, I found it necessary to make the representatives of either party, speak as they formerly felt. If my work should live, it will stand as a beacon, over a bloody sea, to warn our children, when we, who fought upon it, shall have passed away.

J. W. ROGERS.

———· ◄●► ·———

WASHINGTON, D. C.:
THOMAS J. BRASHEARS, PRINTER.
1879.

DRAMATIS PERSONÆ.

————:o:————

President Lincoln and family.
President Johnson.
Madame Surratt.
Annie Surratt.
John Surratt.
Lieutenant Beail.
Lilly Beall.
J. Wilkes Booth.
Edwin Booth.
Agnes Booth.
General Mussy.
Wm. H. Seward.
Payne.
Atzerot.
Herold.
Dr. Mary Trotter.
· Baker & Conger, Detectives.
President Davis.
Robert E. Lee,
        Ghosts, Officers, Soldiers, &c.

DEDICATION.

—— :0: ——

This Drama is inscribed to my friend Frank Golden, of Washington City, a successful merchant, and an honest man. Had fortune blessed him with literary advantages, as nature endowed him with mother wit, and a noble heart; he would have shone as brightly, in letters, as he does in the mercantile and social world.

MADAME SURRATT.

ACT I.

SCENE I—*Road near Arlington—Sentinel on Guard.*

1ST SENTINEL.

More numerous than pigeons, when they cloud
The face of Heaven, by their stormy wings,
Come ghostly couriers, sweeping over head
To Arlington;
And from the bowels of Earth
Grey spirits mount,
To the same dread spot for conference.
Perhaps the war is closing, and those counselors,
Of other generations, taking part,
May now be agitating terms of peace.
Last night they flocked around me; but by
    Heaven!
I would not gaze upon that crowd again—
My hairs on end, and cold drops flaring over me,
For all the pomp and glory of the war.
Their port mysterious, and unsocial eyes,
The smell of coffins, on their midnight robes,
And deep sepulchral voices fright my soul.
    Alarmed at foot falls.   *Enter 2d Sentinel.*
'Tis but the sentinel to take my watch.
Thank God 'twas not that bloodless carravan!
Most welcome, sentinel; you are just in time—
Now, fall asleep as soon as possible.

2D SENTINEL.

Asleep?

1ST SENTINEL.

Aye, post you to the dusky land of nod,
Or sights more terrible than dreams will come.

2D. SENTINEL.

What of that rumor, in the camp—
That ghosts and goblins fright our soldiers here?
Say, sentinel, what time do they appear?

1ST SENTINEL.

Sometimes early; sometimes late they come;
But when the mocking-bird, with dulcet note,
Sweetens the midnight air, and whip-poor-wills
Bewail so piteously, the master's lash.
If suddenly they hush, and in a tone
Of trepidation, cautious and subdued,
Give unlinked harmonics, as in soliloquy,
Then look, and on yon Heights of Arlington,
You'll see whole troops of disembodied spirits.

2D SENTINEL.

To see a ghost hath been my life-long prayer—
My nurses told me of them long ago; ha! ha! ha!
And preachers—ha! ha! ha!—they make their
     living by them.
But say, soldier, have you really seen such?

1ST SENTINEL.

Last night I saw them—Aye, and heard them
     too—
Asses can see their provender, and fools,
Born to be damned—mere brutes, see nothing
     more;
But I was born with a caul on my face,
And, in fact, all lofty souls can see spirits.
They walk about the world most numerous,
When nations tremble, or great States dissolve,
As in Jerusalem, when "they that slept arose"

"And came into the holy city,"
And appeared to many; for those prisoners felt
The Roman Empire shake, when God was on
    the Cross.
There! there they go!—your prayer is answered
    soon—
So follow them; but as for me,
I'll seek a livelier company.

                                        Exit.

2D SENTINEL.

To the limit of my watch will I follow them—
If spies, to capture, and if ghosts, to prove.
O, that I had a silver bullet now!

                                        Exit.

SCENE II. — *Arlington Cemetery — Ghosts of Washington and other American heroes— Federal and Confederate Ghosts — Of Columbus, De Soto and other Discoverers—Pocahontas, Powhattan and other Indian Chiefs—John Brown on side of stage, near the Audience—Music, Star Spangled Banner—Banner 13 Stars, Waving.*

WASHINGTON.

These direful tidings, and this day of blood,
Cry loud to Heaven! and Heaven appoints this
    conference.
Let him who rendered in immortal verse
Our banner—Keys of Maryland—first speak.

ALL.

Keys, Keys—a song from Keys.

KEYS.

When Freedom, crushed and bleeding on the
    ground,
Abandoned every other hope for man,
To Heaven she cried, and Heaven, in pity, gave
This new-born world, uprising from the sea.

Its hills came forth, with kine and cattle crowned,
And all the valleys teemed with jocund song.
Like cowled monks, the misty mountains rose,
To Heaven's high altar, lighted by the stars;
Cecilian thunders leaped along the skies,
And lightnings darted in the face of kings.
Great rivers, flashing to the sun, rolled on;
And solitude stood listening to their cataracts.
Beneath the virgin soil were golden yams,
More luscious than the roots of Ind. or Africa.
Enormous mellons lay upon the ground,
With nectar filled—a banquet for the Gods!
Gigantic birds, unknown to other climes,
With coral neck, and beard upon their breasts,
. Of consequential step and curious gobelins,
Strutted unconscious of a tyrant's power—
A mammoth corn with golden ears was there,
And fruit perennial smiled in every grove.
Upon ten thousand plains fair flowers bloomed,
And o'er them, like the billows of the sea,
Dashed the wild herd of plunging buffalo.
The waves—the waters laughed, and winds sang
    loud,
To Freedom weeping on that distant shore—
Up from the dust she sprang, on whirlwinds
    flew,
To climb the mountains of her own bright
    world—
Thence gazing on her children, all abroad,
And lifting high her standard to the breeze,
She spread her stars upon its ample folds,
And welcomed all the nations of the Earth.
Accursed be he who strikes that banner down!
Thrice cursed her sons who would not lift it up.
Let Death and leanness enter in their ranks,
While Hell gapes wide to take them down!

POWHATAN.

Behold a king—no jewel in his crown,
But feathers from his own imperial bird.
Powhattan salutes ye—Minehaha's Lord,
And Pocahontas' father—cheated of his child,
Who pined and perished in a foreign land—
Behold him standing where his fathers stood—
Ere yet the canting Christian crushed his heart—
Burnt down his wigwam, stole his child,
And murdered Minehaha in her bed.
Truth hast thou told, for once, thou lying
    tongue:
"Upon ten thousand plains, fair flowers bloomed,
And o'er them, like the billows of the sea,
Dashed the wild herd of plunging buffalo."
Those flowers, now drooping with papoosas'
    blood,
And slain, like buffalo, their warlike sires;
But chanting still their war songs as they died.
They cursed your friendship, and your power
    defied.
Well hast thou said, the waters laughed—
Ah, yes, my Minehaha; fare-thee-well!
Thou laughing water; fare-thee-well!
O, my Minehaha! ha! ha! ha!

            Exit, sobbing.
           Exeunt Indians.

JOHN BROWN.

Now stand rebuked thou squeaking trump of
    liberty;
Harken to me, and I will tell thee more.
The red man, and the black man, both are *men*.
Your lofty strain might more become
Some patriot, taught by Christian charity—
Some Wilberforce, or Cowper, when he cried:
"I would not have a slave to till my ground,

To fan me when I sleep, and tremble when I
wake,
For all the wealth of India bought,
Or sinews ever earned."
Vile Anthropophagæ! your fathers all,
Traded in human flesh, poor flesh and blood!
But I was Freedom's first apostle on these
shores,
And struck, at Harper's Ferry, for the rights of
man.

KEYS.

To purchase captives, and to give them homes,
Redeeming them from death, or Pagan rule ;
Was ever merciful; but he who first,
Enslaved the free-born soul, must bear the
mark of Cain.

PATRICK HENRY.

The captive once enthralled, no Christian law
Forbade his changed of masters, nay, sweet
mercy,
Throughout all time, compelled her favored sons,
To buy the captive from a cruel lord—
From Jew or Vandal—Turk or Infidel,
And use his service, for the ransom paid.
T'was thus our Washington, his fuglemen
Restrained, with firm, but gentle hand.
Lo, Washington my witness ! for he soothed,
With lighter chain the captive, driven to his
door.
Aye, by your fathers, driven to Arlington,
Chill-blains upon their feet, and fetters on their
hands,
But like those hemorrhoids, once on Israel sent,
The Blains and fetters now return to you.

WASHINGTON.

Charles Carroll speak.

ALL.

Hear! hear! Charles Carroll, of Carollton,
   hear! hear!

CARROLL.

When freedom first upon these shores unfurled
The banner of the cross, all earth rejoiced.
But lo, a cloud uprising from the sea—
At first no bigger than a prophets hand,
Yet destined soon to burst upon mankind!
England's armadas, staggering on the deep,
Drag Africa in chains across the wave:
And freedom shrieks—commingling her sad
   tears
With thine, O, Cleopatra, falling fast
On Plymoth rock, and freezing as they fall;
For there the slaver packed with dusky forms,
First vomited its curse and slavery on these
   shores;
The *Mayflower* bore them, and her pilgrims
   sang
Loud songs to Liberty, imploring Heaven
To lull the storm, and land each cargo safe.
And when the cable rustled on the shore,
The captives' freedom lost for ever more
Those glorious Pilgrim Saints, all English born,
Rolled their white eyes to Heaven and twanged
   each nasal horn,
Returning thanks, that God had given to that
   shore,
To be baptized, the poor benighted blackamore.
New England's avarice, and her prayerful sons
Transfer the prisoner, to Southern clime;
And take Virginia's gold *their price for blood.*
But all may yet be well; for Heaven is watchful,
Though her children weep—sweet mercy pleads
Before the King of Kings—Pope Urbin too,

And Benedict, on every slaver's mast—
Aye ! though a King should charter it,
Have launched the dreadful curse of Rome.
The prisoner transferred to Southern clime,
May yet be free: for mutual jealousies
Of North and South, may break his chain.
Their rival interests, and the shock of arms—
But not their charity, can shatter it;
For one his service—one his vote—demands—
But see, on yonder heights of Arlington—
One Eagle holds a trembling bird—
Another eagle couching for the prey
Rushes to combat—lo! they fight and die;
But see ! the bird hath mounted to the sky.
Then lift thy standards, freedom, and thy cross
     display.
Peal all thy thunders, let thy cannon peal,
For every chain is shattered, and the bondman
     free.

Music, Hail Columbia.

WASHINGTON.

The storm is passing, and the union saved;
The Blue and Grey shall mingle, side by side;
One Union banner waving over all,
With glory's sentinel to guard our graves,
And keep his watch, till time shall be no more.

*Enter Seceded States, dressed in mourning, each
with a star on her forehead, and a cross, in her
hand.*

1ST STATE.

As deputy for these fair States, I come,
To ask a place upon that glorious banner.

ALL.

Father of our country, hail ! admit us there.

WASHINGTON.

Then lift each cross to Heaven, and swear

To guard that banner, till the day of doom.

ALL.

We swear ! we swear !
Amen ! Amen !

Music, Starspangled Banner.

KEYS.

That cross so glorious on the battle field,
Hath ten fold glory now, in sorrows hand;
Go plant it then, above your glorious dead;
And leave it there, Oh, leave it on those graves,
That heave along like ocean's troubled waves.
Protect it there, 'gainst each invaders hand,
For they are all cradled in their native land.
Perhaps mistaken in their fiery zeal;
But all Americans, true as their steel;
Perchance too zealous for a doubtful right,
But Martyrs to their faith, they fell in fight:
Then twine the wreath, and let your crosses tell,
To coming time, where fruitless valor fell.
Where sleep the brave, who left upon the cliffs
    of time,
Their names immortal, and their deeds sublime.
A moments anger, like the tempest's wrath,
Swept in its fury o'er our country's path.
But there she stands, triumphant o'er the storm,
Our stars and stripes, around her glorious form.
Her sword still red, but lifted high to Heaven,
Proclaims the tempest past, the past forgiven:
Alas ! She weeps, 'tis now her sacred trust,
To watch each warriors grave, and guard his
    dust—
To guard the glory of each soldier's name,
And consecrate it to his Country's fame.
No foreign flag shall wave above her dead,
Nor tyrant foot, nor timid slave shall tread,
Where Canby fought, or Stonewall Jackson bled.

But glory's banner, to their fathers dear,
Shall catch from every wounded heart a tear,
And shine, a rainbow, bright as when it span,
The first wild storm that swept our native land.

WASHINGTON.

Yon morning star, our captain in the sky,
Commands us to retire to our tents.

GENERAL MORGAN.

Stay, stay, regardless of the morning star.
Your loving harmonies are beautiful indeed,
Then hie ye to your green, well-tended graves,
While we return to brushwood and to rocks.
Where vultures tore our flesh and left our bones;
Where weeping mothers seek for us in vain,
And toil as slaves to keep a little life
Still in our baby brothers telling them the tale—
And when our fortunes stolen shall be returned,
And when magnanimous as ye pretend,
The nation gives us graves and hands to tend
    them.
Aye, then; but not till then, our dust can mingle.

JOHN BROWN.

You lie! your fortunes were not stolen--we took
In spoils of war, the gold which ye had coined
From human blood—'Twas I that lead the van,
At Harper's Ferry first I struck for liberty,
When your unequal laws, accursed and hellish,
Did hang me like a dog till dead, dead, dead !
Then all the North was caught into a blaze,
For I was there—(ha! ha! ha!) John Brown was
    marching on,
Your moderate men, as Jackson—ours too---
Such snivellers as Elsworth I detest,
And Lincoln also, a soft hearted fool,
Favors the rebels whom a man of grit
Had hung, and shot as fast as they were caught.

I'd burn the serpents—men and women too,
And send them writhing down to hell,
For trading in human flesh, and turning men to
    beasts.
God gave no property to man; but force
First seized it trampling down the weak,
And weakness yielded to the brave and powerful
So strength prevailed and property arose;
But they who sing *"John Brown is marching on,"*
Will one day raize yon cities from their base—
God speed the day, and hell light up their torches!
New York, Chicago, Pittsburg, and St. Louis, all
Shall have their guilotines, to make France
    tremble—
For her little spirt of blood, was as nothing to
    that glorious sea.
Give me the men who carry fire and sword,
Give me a Morton, Sherman or a Wade,
To sweep with besoms of destruction—
Then go ye rebels to the rocks again
Ye have no country and deserve no graves !

GENERAL MORGAN.

What though we have no country—our fathers,
Lead up by Washington, defended yours,
And struck the British lion at your door:
What tho' their sons should have no graves—
"On fame's eternal camping ground,
Our silent tents, are spread,
And Glory guards, with solemn round,
The bivouac of our dead."

WASHINGTON.

This war of words avail us not;
The Conference is ended—let us Hence.

    Exit.

JOHN BROWN.

Go to, ye snivellers, for I alone,

Rushed single handed on the Devil's own;
And have a right to walk by day, while you
Are frightened by a little morning dew--
A cock can scare ye, but yon morning star
Was my companion at the gate of war--
At Harper's Ferry, o'er the gulches wide,
It led my army to the other side,
Clambering o'er rocks, by cyclops flung,
In some great battle when the world was young
It saw me strike—Aye ! sec's me striking still.
Giving to other men my stuborn will

BOOTH, *passes and Exit.*

There! there! Wilkes Booth! now for a little sport.
I'll make the crater of his soul my fort,
And Freedom's banner, from its heights unfurled,
Shall lead a host of Devils through the world;
For lofty souls, by hellish impulse driven,
Are Hell's best arsenals, when touching Heaven;
And his, though dipped in Heaven's etherial
    blue,
Hath craters vast, for Hell to thunder through;
Then let me seize its heights, and hold the
    while,
Gazing on all beneath with lurid smile;
Then from its pinacles; all stained with blood,
I'll leap into the raging multitude;
And give to working men a higher law,
To hold the world and capital in awe.
Till the Freemen of the North,
Whose children feed on broth,
Light up the avenging fire,
Leaping from spire to spire—
My spirit soaring higher;
Till toiling millions, find their shackles gone,
And shout to Heaven, "John Brown is march-
    ing on."

Enter Booth, and exit.

See, see, he comes again, but paler far
Than when I met him, at the gate of war;
For then a volunteer—most valliant man,
He joined Virginia's troops, to meet my clan—
At Charleston guarded me, and saw me die.
But time avenges every villainy—
What though he live, I have a grudge to take,
Which all the villain's blood can never slake,
Then let me drive him on in crime, till men
Pursue him, like the tiger to his den—
Start at his name, instinctive turning round,
To find a hissing serpent in its sound.
Mothers all trembling—clasping in their arms
Scared infants as his passing shade alarms;
While wrinkled hags, by wolves and witches
    nursed,
Cover their faces at his name accursed.
Rise, rise! ye mantles of the dead, and tear
The womb of time, that I may see him strug-
    gling there.
See! see ! he strikes at yonder towering heads
Whose murdered millions lie in gory beds,
And now prophetic deamons, in their rage,
Ride on the storm—now stoop to yonder stage
And now a prophet's mantle on the air
Shakes pestilence and death—my hangman there
Strikes Lincoln down; and yonder shooting star,
Reveals the last dread tragedy of war !
See, see! the villain comes; but knows it not,
That I have marked the very hour, and spot—
Then rise, ye curtains, of the night and show
The violets withering, where his foot-prints
    glow,
Ye Devils rise and plunge into his soul,
Till the whole world shall shake from pole to
    pole—

But when the deed is done, and darkness
    shrowds the sun,
And Lincoln lies upon his bier,
Pursue the blood-stained murderer,
Still whispering in his ear,
John Brown is marching on—is here !
And when in fire and flame, the villain dies,
Let thunder peals proclaim it through the skies !

Exit.

Enter J. Wilkes Booth.

BOOTH.

Hyperion, like a Chariot all on fire,
Rides up among the stars, and grey cold morning
Ope's once more her eyes on yonder Capitol—
Once more Virginia shakes her clanking chains,
And lifts them up imploringly to Arlington—
Nest of her eagles! once so dear to thee!
O, Liberty! thy cradle and thy tomb!
O, glorious Arlington! Home of a Hero!
Thy festive arches loth to let them die,
Repeated oft the words of Washington,
While Madison, Monroe and Jefferson
Held high discourse on forms of human right;
Or bent the bow, when strung too long,
To ladies fair, in many a social hour!
Here, oft, alas! my own exulting voice
Rang out in childhood's unsuspecting glee—
And other voices calling me to play,
Now silent in their stiff and gory grey.
Ah! yes; the stage is sad, when those we played
    with,
Have all gone to rest! Then hear my vow
Ye murdered and neglected ones, whose bones
Lie bleeching on the hill sides where we played:
Not unavenged, your ghosts shall walk this
    scene—

Envious of the foeman, sleeping in your beds,
And proud to stick their blue plebean noses,
Even in death, beneath the kirchief of a Custis—
To have it said that they were lodged at Arling-
	ton!
Ye, our Fathers—Sons of the South, look down!
And thou, Virginia—mother of Statesmen—
Wake with the morning; but awake to weep!
For your fair bosom, once bedecked wi' flowers,
All brooched and jewelled o'er with golden corn,
Heaves only now with graves — a nation's
	sepulchre!
And thou, my Maryland, dear to this heart,
Look down from yonder hills, and judge me
	kindly,
Like some poor mother, half demented, thou
Dost rock the cradle of thy buried children,
Still muttering thine own immortal poet's song,
Though half the stars have fallen from his
	banner—
I cannot sing that song, but I can perish,
And wrestling—clutching yon strong columns,
I will drag them down, and Dagon's host
Shall perish with me!
Hark! hark! the revelé of yonder camp!
Its rumbling cannon, presage of a storm;
Surcharged with thunder, and the bolts of death
Those clattering horses. and war-bearing mes-
	sengers;
Like vultures balanced on the duky cloud;
That merry marching, measured to the fife,
The drum and trumpet—shouts, and neighing
	steeds,
Proclaim new levies and a countless host,
To batten on the South, already sunk so low—
Nothing but *Intercention* now can save us—

What if mad havock, riding on the air,
Should pluck the tallest tassels of the field!
What if a President and his whole Cabinet
Were taken up the Heaven?—Confusion dire
All order would confound, till France and Eng-
    land
Rocognized the South, and left her children free!
Down busy thoughts! but when I play to-night,
Rhichard the Third shall live within my soul,
And from the furnance of his blasted spirit,
I will snatch a fire brand to light the world—
Will tear this darkness from my native sky,
And set the Southern Cross in glory there!

                                          Exit.

SCENE III—*Same—Road near Arlington—Enter
    Captain Thornton Powel—Cloak over Gray
    uniform, supporting Lilly Beall*

                POWEL.

Come, come, be brave, the worst is over now,
You sail awaits us, and the wind blows fair—
See! see the topmast! how its streamers wave,
And point us to the Capitol. The guards
Can thus be flanked, and your brave brother
    saved—
Once in the city, we can aid him—
Madame Surrat to espouse his cause,
And Booth to plead it with the President—
Come, come, once more be brave; be brave and
    win,
For never yet could prison bar, nor rib of steel,
Withstand the pleadings of an angel's tongue!

                LILLY.

Alas my poor brother—now in chains!
I feel that he can never be exchanged.
You wiser men may little understand it,
But woman's heart is all a prophesy,

And what we know—is only what we feel—
Ah, no, we are too powerless to save him.

Sinks by the road.

O, so weary! frighted all night long,
And trembling more for you, than for myself,
My woman's heart grows faint, and dies within
    me.   .
Thrice have you slain the guards, and thrice
    these hands,
Staunching their wounds, took up the dreadful
    tale.

Lifts up her hands red with blood.

I cannot wash it off, lest, to your soul,
The damning spot should fly—for we are one—
At least were once, till, with an angry grasp,
Unlike your own, you tore me from those offices,
By pity, prompted for a dying foe.
But now we part, for life is ebbing fast,
And life, without you, were worse than death.
But take this rosary, press it to your heart,
And when the flowers of spring shall bloom once
    more
To hide these bloody hands from Heaven, and
    offer
Sacrifices for our sins: O, then remember me!
Go back to camp; you cannot pass yon guard;
Go, Thornton, fight the battles of the South,
And leave me here to die! Farewell! farewell!
Yet swear, before our parting—swear once more,
To love me Thornton, and to keep me in your
    heart.

Taking rosary and twining it on his wrist.

POWEL.

We'll have no parting yet; but let me swear,
And on a soldier's sword, (*draws*,) and by the
    stars,

Dumb witnesses, whose soft and dewy eyes
Have looked through Southern bowers on our
 love,
And by yon mocking-bird, rehearsing it
To roses, bent upon their tearful boughs;
And by the moon, whose silvery bow in Heaven,
Was snatched by Cupid when he made us one—
One heart—one soul—one life, and one Eternity!
I swear to love thee; and to save thy brother!

    LILLY—*Rising.*

Those words, like nectar, poured into my soul,
Supply new strength—now I can go,
For gentle words to woman's heart, are more
Than all the pomp and glory of the world!
Lead on! and I will follow thee,
Though tempests, rave and torrents sweep our
 path!

    POWEL, *kissing her.*

Remember love, our new-born names—
Yours Lilly Boyd—mine Payne—remember,
 Payne!
For Beall and Powel would betray our colors.

       Exeunt.
    Voice behind the scenes.

    1ST SENTINEL.

Halt! halt!

 Sentinel fires—Clash of arms—They fight back
to the stage and around it—Sentinel falls

    PAYNE.

O, that the wrongs and ruins of the South
Were centered in this arm—its thunderbolt
That struck thee down, should strike the North
 as well,
And quench, with blood, the very fires of Hell!

       Exit.

SCENE IV.—*Richmond—Before the President's Mansion—Enter soldiers, and citizens serenad-ing.*

1ST CITIZEN.

That's Jeff. Davis' house. Come, let's give him Dixie.

2D CITIZEN.

Let's call him out, and have a speech first.

3D CITIZEN.

No, no, Dixie first, and then the speech.

4TH CITIZEN.

We want no Dixie now—first for the speech—
And if he brings good news from Lee or Long-street,
Then we'll have Dixie; but they say that Peters-burg
Has fallen—first make him tell the news—
And then if good, wind up with Dixie—
But if the news be bad, we'll shake him for it.
Damn if I don't lead the crowd to make him squeal.

OFFICER.

Peace! Peace? vile braggart! you carpet bag!
You d—d tobacco speculator—fool!
You wore a cockade; but never fired a gun.
And your vile crowd have brought us to this pass.
Dare you to criticise and underate
The foremost man of all his time?
Why, Yankeedom and the whole South once vied
To stamp him current for the bank of fame!
And you to flip, and ring his metal—bah!
Were you in Mexico? at Monterey?
At Buena Vista? Where did you enlist?
Our forlorn hope, he lead at Monterey.
I saw him mounting Fort Diabolo,

Throttling the cannon—daring death—
Our starry banner waving in his hand
Like wingéd seraphim defying war!
Begrimmed with powder, and besmeared with
  blood,
He bore it upward--onward—Monterey was
  won!
"And there he stood, an Eagle in the sun."
At Buena Vista next our cause seemed lost—
Taylor and Brag were yielding to the storm:
When fresh as condors, from the mountain
  heights,

Rushed down ten thousand lancers on our left.
There stood Jeff. Davis—Mississippi's sons
His hope of victory—lo! they seem to fly.
His center first retiring, 'til it formed
Into an open V; but while each branch
Of that dread letter on the field of blood,
Seemed to retreat; and thus drew in the foe,
As flies into the yawning crockodile;
He halted suddenly, and faced about;
His Mississippi rifles blazed along each line;
And like a bosky hill, bathed in the sun,
Or mound mysterious, rising in those wilds—
Or rather like a hill of blasted pines,
Those Lancers--and their shattered lances lay—
Jeff. Davis master of the field;
And glittering on the heights of fame!
Wild with delight, a glorious nation then
Her preferments and honors proffered him;
Her power supreme, to hold the helm of war,
She gave into his hands, her record –his!
Then Senator, he scorned and held at bay,
Like a great mountain, standing in the sea,
The raging billows of fanatic strife—
'Til warning them in vain, his hope had fled;

And now tho' battling 'gainst the world in arms,
He leads the land of Washington to war.
For four long years, undaunted and sublime,
He stands—the brightest mark upon the cliffs of
    Time!
        Soilders—Huzza! Huzza! Huzza!
Davis! Davis! Davis! Huzza! Huzza! Huzza!
        Enter Davis on Balcony.

FELLOW CITIZENS :—It always gives me pleasure to meet you, for I know your devotion to the cause of liberty and to the sovereignty of States.

Greece in her palmiest day, was a great Confederate government—as such, she fought at Thermopolae Plataea, and Salamis: nor ever yielded to domestic or foreign tyrants, until her sovereign States succumbed to Federal power. You, fellow soldiers, and fellow citizens, are fighting for States' rights, and for State sovereignty, guarded by Constitutional authority. You are fighting against Federal power, a mere creature and servant of the States--Your cause is just, and millions of brave men throughout the North now shackled by the grip of war, are with you. They hold as you do, that no aggregation of States—no vast mob of many nations—no raging commune should dictate to a free born people, and enslave their sons. What though we fail in battle, these brave men, inspired by your example, will yet sustain the cause for which your sons are bleeding. Remember the real issue—slavery was only an exciting element, trumped up by cunning demagogues to lead the mob. They know, full well, that our slaves are by far the happiest peasantry on earth —better, in their condition now, than when

driven by Yankee masters; from whom our fath
ers purchased them; and this the negroes understand; they also understand that their condition
is infinitely better than that of many white slaves,
of the North; some of whose masters so cruelly
oppress them. Then let us keep to the issue—
the sovereignty of States—and should our last
army go down in battle, our cause will still
survive. The whole world now combined
against us, may conquer on the field. But the
brave and true men of the North, threatened by
a raging commune will clamor for Constitutional safeguards; and be compelled to call our
sons, in peaceful armor—or, if need be, with the
sword—perhaps ourselves—to fight for Constitutional liberty, and for the rights of man.

Fellow citizen and fellow soldiers, I bid you
good night.

ALL.

Huzza! Huzza! Huzza!

Exeunt.

ACT II.

SCENE 1.—*President's Mansion.—Lincoln reading M. S. S.—Music—John Brown, in the distance.*

LINCOLN.

We want no commune here—want no secession
  neither—
No John Brown marching on, nor squealing
  Dixie;
Except it be to play them for a little sport—
Keys was a Southern man, and born in Maryland,
And his "Star Spangle Banner" will be played,
With Hail Columbia, till the day of doom.
For golden songs descending to a nation,
Make through all time her best inheritance;
And the recreant wretch, who could relin-
  quish them,
So dear to his fathers, whether North or South,
And in a corner, like a cricket chant,
"John Brown is marching on," or "Dixie"—
O, I have no patience with such men !
So when the commune bawl, or Southern fool
Sticks a cockade upon his fiery breast;
I know the fitful storm must pass away;
Impartial men, on either side, will lead
The people and return ere long to union.
So let the fools rip, a day is near at hand,
When reason can be seated on her throne,
And this great union, snatched from ruin,
Our stars and stripes shall float along the sky,
Wherever the sun shines or waters roll !

Secession is a thing, most foul and pitiable,
A kind of cross-eyed, ill contrived abortive- ·
Ben Butler in another form; but uglier—
A blot, upon the North, as well as on the South—
A rope of sand, disintegrated from the start--
The laughing stock, and jest of all mankind !
Never were sane men so thoroughly misled,
As they who clamor for secession—
Whether in Massachusetts or in Carolina,
For Massachusetts first conceived the monster,
And her grim legislature, gave it birth.
Jeff Davis took it to his arms, and now
The whole world trembles in its presence.
T'is but the commune in another form—
States riding on the storm's of human passion,
Poor John Brown marching on, and nothing else.

Enter a messenger, bearing dispatches—Lincoln reads them.

Well, the Rebellion drags along, and though
Its back is broken, still its fiery fangs
Are dangerous as ever, and its rattling tail
Forewarns that they may "fight to the last ditch;"
And fight they will, if driven to despair—
If we insist on blotting out their States,
And turning them to Provinces--if soldiers
Must be kept to garrison their homes;
And men, like Butler, give those soldiers leave,
For fancied insults, or a scornful look,
To make their daughters women of the town,
By heavens ! they'll fight it out, and I would too.
Now some would burn and crucify the South,
Beechers and Brownlows, and a host of saints.
All preaching love, to cut Confederate throats.
But I myself was born in old Kentucky,
And have a soft place in my heart for her.
My dear old mother sleeps among her hills,

My fathers too all sleep in Old Virginia,
And her greatest statesmen have been my
    friends,
But *"by the eternal Gods,"* as Jackson said,
"I'd hang them high as Haman to preserve this
    Union."
Yet could we make an honorable peace,
The South should have protection, and return
To join us in a great regenerated country.
Freedom to all, inscribed upon our banner,
And in our hearts "forgiveness for the past."
"Malice to none; but charity for all."
And when this tempest shall have passed away
The mystic chords of memory stretched,
From every soldier's grave, to every heart
In this great land, shall swell the pean of our
    victory !

Exit.

SCENE II—*President's grounds—Enter Dr. Mary
Trotter in male attire—Beecher meeting her.*

DR. MARY.

O, Mr. Beecher : Mr. Beecher, how fortunate to
Meet you here. Come now, introduce me to the
    President.

BEECHER.

Certainly—He'll be here in a moment—
Dr. you are looking remarkably well--
See, there he comes !

Lincoln approaches.

BEECHER.

Allow me to present you, Mr. President,
Our great Surgeon, Dr. Mary Trotter—

LINCOLN.

Indeed ! I'm glad to meet you Dr. Mary,
So Dr., you cut soldiers legs off, Eh? ha! ha! ha!

But dont you feel queer, when you cut a man ?
 ha ! ha ! ha !
Take care Dr. that you don't get your own leg
 broke.
For then you'll have to send for Beecher.

DR. MARY.

No need of sending, he'll be sure to come,
Like a good pastor—loving all his lambs !
But Mr. President I came from Ford's,
To ask your Cabinet to Booth's great play.
Here are the invitations—ten in number.

Giving them.

O, he's an angel, sir—almost a God—
And all the women of the town are crazy for
 him.

LINCOLN.

I hope you are not a woman of the town—

DR. MARY.

O, yes I am, but hold to woman's rights—

LINCOLN.

Take care that you don't hold to something else,
For Booth would make you change your politics,
And if you married him—one thing I know,
He'd have them breeches off, and make you wear
 a frock.
Good bye !—Good bye !—ha ! ha ! ha !

DR. MARY,

No, sir; I'll wear them to the bitter end—

Exit.

LINCOLN—*Laughing.*

Beecher, which is her bitter end?

BEECHER

Perhaps, your excellence, she means her latter
 end,
A most important thing; for all must die—
The cares of State, the corronet and crown—

Upheavings of a mighty land like this,
And of our little bosoms—all must sink,
To rest, and be forgotten in the grave.
Then "the true inwardness" must all come out.
To me, to you—and all of us, that day
Approaches like a thief—"nest hiding" then—
Our loves and hates, and all our little schemes,
Will leave us "on the ragged edge," of time—
Each in his narrow bed and married to the
    worm !

Exeunt.

SCENE III.—*Booth's room in Washington—Portraits on the wall of the Booths, Beall, and Lilly*
BOOTH.

Richard was a villian "of the whole cloth ;"
And sweet relenting nature never touched
A single chord in his abandoned bosom.
He slew alike the innocent and guilty,
To make their trunks his stepping-stones to power ;
This I was never formed for, but by Heaven !—
As Curtius leaped into a gulf, so I,
To saved my native land, would plunge
Into the seething chauldron of a nation's wrath—
Nor Heaven, nor earth, nor hell could pluck me
    thence;
But 'ere one leaps into a gulf, perhaps—
'Twere well to write some record on the cliff,
That they who come hereafter may devine,
What hopes he built upon, and why he fell.

Writes letter to Clark and leaves it on table.

Yes, in the fiery tempest that must rise,
Naught less than miracles could save me;
Lascivious Fortune then, to Judas turned,
May crack upon my cheeks; but I will hurl
Her kisses back to meet their swords and staves,
And fall, at last, if fall I must,

Like Brutus—not sustained by Senators—
No! not like Brutus, with an host of friends,
Creeping behind the kisses of a Casca, no!
But like Niagara, all alone in power,
One patriot soul shall leap upon the gulf,
And leave eternal rainbows where it plunged!
Not sixty Senators to vanquish Cæsar,
But one strong arm to prop a falling cause—
Like Brutus striking for the rights of man,
Perhaps like Brutus, on the plains of Philipi,
Weltering in blood, despairing and abandoned,
Traduced, and scorned, and hated for the time
That Cæsar's armies parcelled out the world;
Yet living on and honored by mankind;
So be't; and when the world forgets a Brutus,
Then, but not till then, my fame shall die;
For I will live when yonder dome shall piece-
      meal fall,
When yonder trumpets to the judgment call,
And ruin writes the epitaph of all !

                    Enter Thornton Powel.

Why, Thornton Powel, Heavens! how came you
here?
How pass their lines! what news, my boy?
                    POWEL.
How pass their lines!   I have a ready tongue,
Whose thirsty edge, (*drawing bloody sword,*)
      lapping the blood of dogs
For three contentious nights, can answer you.
Challenged at every turn, pursued, hemmed in,
And fighting inch by inch, this, my best friend,
Procured our passage hither!
                    BOOTH.
What from our army?   What news, my boy?
                    POWEL.
My grey-haired sire—God! can it be true?

Pursuit being vain, they sought my father's
    house,
And slew him, helpless, pleading for his life.
My sisters, then, to save themselves from shame,
Lucretia's guiltless dagger seized and died;
I saw it not—yet see it standing there—
You blazing roof! the tears and blood that fell,
Freeze me with horror while the tale I tell.

BOOTH.

Horrible! most horrible! Oh, it was
A dark and damnèd—most infernal deed;
Yet, they who perish now, are Fortune's
    favorites,
Nursed in a quiet cell, protected, safe,
And mingling with the dust for which they died.
Unused to fawning, your Virginia blood
Could never crawl and creep as things do here.
Better to die and bid the world farewell,
To stride the withers of some windy blast,
And ride through lightnings to the gate of
    Heaven,
Than lick a master's hand for place and power.
O, I do hate the creeping things called men—
And most those Southern men who skulk and
    cringe—
The smell of mules and negroes they delight in;
But powder scares them, and the villains crawl.
Take comfort then—cheer up—'twill all be well.
What from our army? What from Lee?
What of the truce at City Point?

POWEL.

All overtures for peace have been rejected,
And our bleeding army, stung to their wounds
By base conditions offered, flew to arms.
I fear that all is over—our base is cut,
And Sheridan goes raiding in the rear;

Lee struggles like a storm-tossed vessel stranded,
When every billow sweeps her groaning deck;
God only knows how long he'll weather it!

BOOTH.

Then shall we have another act to play !
Rome's Campus Martins, with her three con-
    spirators,
Shall take the stage in Washington. What think
    you?

POWEL.

You speak in parables.   Speak out,
For I was always blunt—perhaps too frank.
Speak out and show the bottom of your mind.

BOOTH.

Richard the Third is on the boards to-night,
And you shall learn the lesson while I play.

POWEL.

Impossible, for I return to-night.

BOOTH.

Whither?

POWEL.

To my command.

BOOTH

Then wherefore did you come?

POWEL—*Pointing to Lilly's Picture.*

T' escort that lady.

BOOTH.

What! Lilly Beall? and is she here?

POWEL.

At Madame Surratt's; but we have changed our
    names.
Remember to call her Lilly Boyd; as for me,
My name is Payne.   Be sure to get it right,
For should the bloodhounds scent my track,
They'd hang me for a spy.

BOOTH.

A halter would then take the place of Lilly's
    arms.
O, that I, too, could have so fair a gibbet!
For one less beautiful might soon be mine!
Say, why this risk, and wherefore did she come?

PAYNE.

Of course you know her brother has been cap-
    tured?

BOOTH.

Lieutenant Beall?   No, not a word; come, tell it
    me.

PAYNE.

Captured, beyond all doubt, and t'escort his
    sister.
I come on furlough; but return to-night,
And you should see her to New York,
Where she expects to find him.

BOOTH.

By Heaven! he's dearer to this love—lack heart
Than all my kindred—brothers, sisters—all,
Except my mother and my murdered friends.
Captured, you tell me?   Where and when?

PAYNE.

Some telegrams we sent will soon be answered,
And you shall know to-night what prison holds
    him.
My time is short.   Take Lilly to your charge;
I have a long and dangerous road before me.
       Going, shakes hands.   Good-night.
  BOOTH—*Holding Powel Confidingly.*

Stay! stay!
When you return to camp, remember this—
And should it happen, say "I told you so"—
Mark well my words, and pin them to your heart.

Defeats are sometimes turned to victory;   •
A single arm can sometimes turn the tide of war.
Now, I am hatching up a bran new play;
Be ready for your part; take Brutus if you like.

POWEL.

O! that a Brutus could be moulded now,
And leaping from the fiery furnace of this war,
Bring curses down upon his towering head,
From hypocrits and villains to the end of time!

BOOTH.

Say, Powel, did you know that Brutus was a
     coward?

POWEL.

"He was the noblest Roman of them all."

BOOTH.

Aye, but his gizzard was so thin of grit
That Cassius was required to grind its purpose,
Else, had its blunted edge proved most abortive;
And, to speak truly, mine needs whetting too;
But you could grind it, Powel, to such keenness
That it would rip the very womb of time,
And send great spirits thro' to Heaven—yea;
Could cleave the dome of yonder Capitol.
Come, tell me, Powel, do you see anything?
Look in my eye; behold your image there.

     *Holding his hand, puts the other arm around
him.*

Perhaps our hearts, now laid together thus,
And linked so long in boyhood's trustful love,
Like shells, by Tyrant Neptune cast ashore—
Might whisper "vengeance"--"Brutus," "Cas-
     sius"—Rome."

     POWEL—*Releases himself.*

Would God that I were Cassius, and could find
A Brutus bold enough to strike my palm!

BOOTH---*Striking palms.*

Soft! soft!   Now, should our armies fail, do you
Mount as Virginius did, and ride to Rome—
The very valleys shouting to your horse's hoofs—
Virginia's valleys shouting back to Heaven:
"*Sic Semper Tyranis!*" Rome is free!

POWEL.

How shall I read, in all this trash,
The purpose of your soul.   Speak out.

BOOTH.

What if the President were sent to Heaven,
Would France and England recognize the South?

POWEL.

If Cerberus should meet me in the way,
I'd off with both his heads, while you forsooth,
Would decolate but one, to make the dog more
      hideous.

BOOTH.

No dread of law?   No qualms of conscience, eh.

POWEL.

Conscience and law?   Yes, these shall point the
      way,
As taught us by the statesmen of our day.
"*A higher law*" has lately been proclaimed,
As better far than what our fathers framed;
Seward proclaimed it; Lincoln holds it good,
To fill the world with misery and blood.
"That higher law" deprived us of the slaves,
Our fathers purchased from the canting knaves,
Because forsooth we would not wear the chain
Of tarriffs, levied only for their gain.
They crushed State-rights, to make that claim
      secure,
Then gave to Federal power what States pos-
      sessed before,
And having numbers—Vandals from afar—
3

"Cried havoc and let slip the dogs of war."
Down came their armies, and the fiends accursed,
Our homes invaded with infernal lust.
From blazing roofs our helpless women driven,
Made suicide their last appeal to Heaven,
Imploring God, yet tearing wide their wounds,
At sight of which o'er sickened nature swoons.
All this and more the conscience justifies,
If we may trust their snivelling and their lies.
That "HIGHER LAW," a mask for crime,
To suit the pious knavery of our time,
Command me then, and if our armies fail,
That higher law shall over might prevail.
Prepare your play, and put me in the cast,
For I will fight, and fight them to the last.

Exit.

BOOTH.

His heart was gentle as his love for Lilly,
Ere this unnatural war had tongued its wounds;
And yet to the tiger's fierceness could it rise
When o'er topping insolence presumed too far,
I well remember how he struck a giant once,
For giving insults to a helpless woman,
First with his hand; but drawing then his sword,
He clove the villain to his buttox.
With three such men, knit firmly to my soul,
This drama could be played; but without such,
'Twould drag upon the stage, and prove abortive;
Yet every actor cannot be a star,
And I must cast this piece for humbler stock.

Knocks.
Enter Harold, dressed gaily with flowers.

HAROLD.

They say that we are wonderously alike.
"Now is the winter of our discontent
Made glorious summer by the Son of York"—

BOOTH.

Come, butterfly, if I should blow a candle out,
Could you blow out another?
Tell Atzerot to come in here.

Exit Harold.

This shallow boy will ape me to the last;
And like the monkey, shaving as his master,
The poor thing, ere long, may vent his windpipe.
Vain of my friendship, he would die to serve me,
While Atzerot, for money, would encounter h—ll;
And yet I scarcely fancy thus with murderers
To conspire. What is conscience after all?
Perhaps the ghost of early training throws
Its shadow on the path of desperate deeds,
Or creeps behind to hold the elbow back.
O, coward conscience, trembling at a nightmare!
Poor spaniel, pawing at thy master's door!
Vile shadow, cast by some obtrusive light—
Ah, yes, a light! and that is what we dread—
A light more piercing than th' unpupiled eye
Of day—burning like phosforous in bones—
Unseen and covered by the womb of darkness,
Yet giving keenness to the stings of memory,
And penetrating every chamber of the soul;
Let him who boasts his freedom bawl with fools;
But all of us are slaves and cowards from the
        start!

Enter Herold and Atzerot—Booth abstracted.

ATZEROT.

Vell Master Booth, vy did you send for me?

BOOTH.

Not now, not now, eh; some other time will do.
For I, eh, am going; but both of you, eh, re-
        member,
I'll need your services some other time—
Yours, Atzerot, for money—Harold, yours,

For love.   Both meet me here to-morrow night.

ATZEROT.

Vell, de best time for anyting is now.

BOOTH.

No, no; not now; some other time; some other
time.

ATZEROT.

Vell, shentlemens, mit money you can buy me,
For I can cut dem throats as good as any man.

BOOTH.

Why do you speak of cutting throats?

HAROLD.

He takes us both for murderers.

ATZEROT.

Yes, shentlemens, I listened mit de key-hole
Ven you and Pain vas fightin fur de last;
Mine Got, I knows it all—give me de monish;
Tells me vat fur do—gives me de knife,
An' tells me who, fur dead men's tells no tales!

BOOTH.

Begone, base cut-throat. Go! begone, begone!
Aside.
O, how the villain freezes up my blood.

ATZEROT—*Going.*

Vell, you sent fur me, and I can go;
But if I tells de policeman, vat fur den?
And Dr. Mary Trotter—vat for her?
She listens mit de key-hole, too! ha, ha;
Vat if she tell de President! vot den!
Some tings, you bet, I don't likes pretty well.

Going.

BOOTH.

Stay, stay; my blood was frozen by your villainy;
But meet me, in the green-room, when the play

Shall warm it. Then will I cast your several parts.

Exit H. and A.

As they go out John Brown rises with serpents over Booth's head.

Booth looking at his watch.

'Tis just an hour ere the play begins;
But Richard shall be aped as ne'er before on
    earth,
For I will fit the deep intents of his dark soul,
So nicely to mine own, that all shall cry.
" 'Tis he! 'tis he! My father's ghost once more;
Shall put the Buskin on—his fathers too,
Shall stride the stage, and fill my soul
With all the fiery vengeance of our race.

Enter Dr. Mary Trotter.

What, again obtruding! Woman, go, go.
Take back your letter with it sickening vows—
It's baby--puking of immodest love.

DR. MARY—*Snatching it.*

Then give it me, and learn that woman's wrath
Hath ten-fold fury for her love.

Reads aside.

Mary E. Surratt, aha!—a pretty thing to love!

Aside, reads.

Remember your promise to write or come early;
John will be off to Richmond in the morning.
Aha! From home. The widow there?

To Booth.

And you to spurn me for a wrinkled hag!
The strumpet; I'll tear her very eyes out;
The Rebel wench; I'll hang her on a gibbet,
And you shall dangle by your lady love.
The hag! Ill give you both a swinging hammock
For your marriage bed. I'll—I'll—

BOOTH.

I cannot bear your costume; and your face,

Pecks like a hawk, into my very soul.
Whether man or woman, what e'er thou art,
Monster—I cannot brook your presence—go!

DR. MARY.

Now mark me Traitor, I will have your heart.
Since beauty cannot win it, fury can;
For I will clutch it in these polycarpal bones,
And hurl it down, and stamp it in the dust,
Or snatch it on my cane, and swing it high,
Then will I hang it in the market place,
To be pecked at by hawks, and vultures tamed
To loyal citizens, since men have turned to beasts.
Go, Traitor; scheme with Atzerott and Payne;
But I will put detectives on your track.
Ha! ha! I'll have your heart, ha! ha! ha! ha!
And her's—her eyes—her heart—her neck with
    yours.
Ha! ha! ha! ha!

Exit.

BOOTH.

Poor doubled sexed, and most unnatural thing—
Essence of Yankee impudence and guile;
I'll play my part so boldly, and with art
So like to Tarquin Brutus, that your charge
Shall fly to chaff. A pretty thing to love!
Crow-footed Time now clawing at her temples;
The shadow of his wing upon her cheek,
And his black beak bent down between her eyes—
That forked costume, too. O, hideous!
But I am wasting gaslight on too poor a thing.

Turns off the gas

Richard now waits to don me with his hump,
To breath his fiery vengeance in my soul,
And I will lead his ghastly crowd to crimes,
Unaudited in these most Christian times;
When Tyrants, in the gorgon mask of law,

Our kindred slay, to hold the world in awe,
We, too—without a mask—on Freedom's heights
Will strike them down, and perish with our
       rights!   *Exit Booth.*
SCENE IV.—*Booth's Room—Beall's and Lilly's
  Portraits on the Wall—Enter Conger and Baker,
  Detectives.*

BAKER.

Are you quite sure that this is his room?

CONGER.

No, not sure.

BAKER.

Well, I am sure of one thing.

CONGER.

What's that?

BAKER.

Why; that we detectives might be shot
As well as other men.

CONGER.

And Booth is a dead shot with a pistol.

BAKER.

Let's be sure—strike a light.

CONGER.

O, no danger—his play won't be out for two
hours yet.   He plays Richard the Third to-night;
and that's a long play.   Besides, Dr. Mary
brought us to the door, and of course she knows
his room.   *Striking a light.*
Yes, no mistake, this is it.

BAKER.

How do you know?

CONGER.

That's his picture there, and there's the picture of Lieut. Beall.   And that's Beall's sister,
the girl we saw at Madame Surratt's—now be
quick; this is his room; let's go through it.
                    Pulling open the table draw.

BAKER.

Hold on; these pictures might give some clue.
Tell me again. Who is this Beall?

CONGER.

Why, he's the fellow they captured raiding on
St. Albans. A captain of artillery. First with
Stonewall Jackson—now a Lieutenant in the
Confederate Navy.

BAKER.

Lieutenant Beall, you say? The same our
dispatches spoke of?

CONGER.

The very same—condemned to be shot or
hanged next Friday. That's his sister. Both
infernal rebels.

BAKER.

But tell me—what of this Booth?

CONGER.

Why, he's the great actor.

BAKER.

Fool! I know that; but what about his antece-
dents. You can't shadow a man properly till
you know all about him.

CONGER.

His forefathers, for generations past,
Have been the greatest actors on the stage.
Descended from the Jews, they still inherit
Those gifts of genius, energy and thrift,
Which make Judea's name a proverb thro' the
    world;
And notwithstanding England's cruel prejudice,
She cradles them in old West Minster Abbey.
His father was a wonder on the stage—
And J. Wilkes Booth inherits all his genius.

BAKER

What kin is he to Edwin Booth?

CONGER.

I'll take that back, for Edwin is his brother;
And both stars of the first magnitude.
The glory of our stage.

BAKER.

O, I know Edwin Booth, and he knows me;
But I always took him for an Englishman.

CONGER.

No, not he; they're all to the manor born;
All born in Maryland.   Their mother still
Presides in the old homestead, and they have
Sisters, and another brilliant brother, named—
I think his name is Junius Brutus Booth—
And, on their mother's side, they claim affinities
With General Lee—the Powels, Bealls and Mad-
    isons—
All families of great note in old Virginia—
But Edwin is a Union man.

BAKER.

Now I see it all—be quick.
Let's go through the papers.
    *They rummage in drawers and scatter letters on
floor—Baker at Bureau, and Conger reads letters
at table.*

BAKER.

Here are a thousand letters from the women.

CONGER.

Yes, they are all crazy for him, ha! ha! ha!
Hear this.   Ha! ha! ha! ha! *Reads.*
"I have read of Gods in history, but never
Saw one till you played last night," ha! ha! ha!
"Let me but bow down and kiss your footprints.
They make the very ground burn with glory.
Then spurn me, if you can.   This will be my
last letter.   If you should not answer it, I will

call at your hotel, this evening, to demand it."
Ha! ha! ha!

BAKER,

Reading letter left on table, during Conger's reading.

I knew it!   Hell's to pay!

Reads: "To J. S. Clark, Theatrical Manager, Philadelphia."

CONGER.

Clark is his brother-in-law.

BAKER—*Reads.*

"Dear Clark, our once bright stripes look like bloody gashes on the face of Heaven."

CONGER.

That sounds like craziness.

BAKER—*Reading on.*

I know how foolish I shall be deemed for taking such a step as this, where on one side I have many friends, and everything to make me happy, where my profession alone has gained me an income of more than $20,000 a year, and where my great personal ambition in my profession has such a great field for labor.   On the other hand, the South has never bestowed upon me one kind word—a place where now I have no friends, except beneath the sod—a place where I must either become a private soldier or a beggar.   To give up all the former for the latter, besides my mother and sisters, whom I love so dearly,(although they differ from me so widely in opinion,) seems insane; but God is my judge   Right or wrong, God judge me, not man.   For be my motive, good or bad, of one thing I am sure, *The lasting condemnation of the North.*   I love peace more than life. Have loved the Union beyond expression.   For four years have I waited, hoped, prayed for the dark clouds to break and for a restoration of our former sunshine. To wait longer would be a crime. All hope for peace is dead. My prayers have proved as idle as my hopes. God's will be done. I go to see and share the bitter end."*

CONGER.

You can't make anything out of that.

BAKER.

I can't, eh?

CONGER.

No, he talks the same way to Lincoln himself.

BAKER.

Then Lincoln's a fool—that's all.

Exeunt.

Enter Miss Agnes Booth.

AG. BOOTH.

Alas! this news falls heavily. My brother
Almost sank beneath it; and Lilly Beall—
Poor child! her moaning haunts me still.

Enter Edwin Booth.

Edwin, Edwin; where is Wilkie?

E. BOOTH.

Not yet returned?

A. BOOTH

Not yet, Edwin; have you seen him since?

E. BOOTH.

Only a moment, when he rushed out from the
    stage.
This acting Richard always makes him mad—
More reckless than father, when he played his
    Brutus;
But I never saw him half so wild before—
And then to make the matter worse, that news

*[This letter is preserved in Townsend's letters to the New York Sun.]

From poor Lieutenant Beall, afflicts him sorely.
You must to bed, Agnes; I shall find him soon.

Exeunt.

*(Same Scene—Booth's Room—Enter Wilks Booth
—Glances at Letters on the Floor.)*

W. BOOTH.

Well, the play is ended, and ended well.
Richard no longer now affects the stage,
And vanished, like a dream, are all his actors;
Yet still on many a weary couch, where sleep
Begets fantastic images, more real,
They play the King, and those unhappy
        children—
Their auditors, whose just applause inspired,
Gone with them to mysterious and oblivious
        realms,
Now play unconsciously their several parts—
Mere mimicry of that eternal sleep,
When the great closing scenes shall be adjusted,
And the last curtain falls!
O that I, too, could sleep! but I cannot.
Thou, Lieutenant Beall, condemned to die.
Thou cans't not sleep, and why should I!
But the current of war must have its course,
And we poor pismires can only peep up
At the spurs, of our booted and brave masters.
They call it liberty, and yet invade
All that is sacred in the rights of man.
Home is no longer private, and even love's
        whispers
Are blown through trumpets to the giggling
        crowd.
'Tis not the people of that mighty nation,
For whom our fathers took Cornwallis' sword—
On old Virginia's soil—and paid her blood.
No; the people are ever friends to liberty;

But base politicians—both North and South—
Have driven us to this verge of ruin.
Black weeds of mourning darken all the land;
Millions of orphans, wailing thro' the night,
Ask for their fathers, to be answered by a tear;
And other millions, born to purple, now
To poverty reduced, shiver with cold,
While low-born insolence rides over them.
O, my country! land of the free, farewell!
And thou, my Maryland, O, my Maryland!
Thy hearthstones shattered and thy children
    slain—
Farewell! *Turning to Beall's Picture.*
'Twas a fond impulse to return to thee,
Poor shadow of a thousand manly virtues!
Who would not stand abashed before such
    majesty!
And all the more in this room, with its memories.
Aye; this chamber, graceless as that garden,
Where the vile serpent coiled our mother Eve,
And slimed those flowers fresh from God's own
    hand—
This chamber, shiftless as a country stage,
Where revellers drank down the beaded hours,
Sparkling for better purposes, and where
Bright eyes and swimming forms, like th' un-
    frocked wind,
Unheralded and unattended, came and went.
O, conscience, conscience; would that I could
    slay thee!
O, for some talisman to conjure back
Thy clattering horses, unrelenting time!
             Enter young girl richly attired.
What, so young, so fair, so beautiful!
Perhaps high-born, and to some mother tied
By sunbeams, twisted from a father's brow.

4

Poor child! are these thy letters? Take them back.

Gives letters.

Go, go! Go to some cloister, child, and wed,
With your imagination, Heaven's sweet Prince—
Not Richard—he's an arrant rake, a murderer.
Go throw thyself upon that mother's heart again,
And suck once more the flowers of Paradise;
But fly those painted men you see upon the stage.
We are not formed to love as angels love.
I have a sister, too—a mother—go, go!
Me thought those letters came from some enthu-
     siast,
Tutored in the world's arts, and fit for me;
But now I quake to find thee on that crater;
Fly! or hell will suck thy childish feet.

Exit girl.
Turning to Beall's picture.

O, my brave friend! From thee I learned such
     lessons,
As high-born souls and chivalry impart.

Turning to Lilly's Picture.

And thou, sweet angel, shining on my soul,
As lillies that cup up the riplets of the lake,
To shed their sweetness o'er its garnished waters,
So thou did'st drink some surface of my better
     self,
Unconscious of the horrid depths that lie beneath!
O, I must fly this chamber with its memories.
I'll seek again the midnight stage:
Which suits the purpose of my darkened soul—
The midnight stage! So like to death itself!
Perhaps my murdered friends might meet me
     there;
And other spirits, cutting through the curtain,
May gleam upon me, like ten thousand swords.
Why not? They walked from Paradise to Calvary!

All ages—all great intellects beheld them.
Even Socrates, Earth's prime Philosopher,
Had a familiar spirit; tho' fools laughed.
So hucksters, in Jerusalem, and Athens,
Giggled in the temples, as now they do.
Devils have made assaults on human souls,
And shaped themselves to every form—
From writhing serpent, up to man's estate.
Angels in Gethsemane, 'tis said,
Appeared to Christ, and bore a cup to strengthen
    him.
The Devil, too, once hurled him high in air,
And placed him on a pinnacle of God's great
    temple—
Thence to a lofty mountain, and arrayed
Before him all the kingdoms of the world!
Was every age made up of knaves and villains?
Or is our little span the only one,
Unworthy visits from th' unseen world?
Or are we such pedlers, and base shop-keepers,
That like the meaner sort of olden time,
We see no spirits—our noses stuck in samples.
No, no; mere hucksters never saw the stars—
Much less th' invisible host which they portend.
Stars, are but shadows, cast by spirits close to
    God;
And such are serpents, too, by Devils formed.
Ah! yes, great goblins, of the ancient globe,
Do walk about this world; and I will meet them
On that same stage where Richard fell to-night—
Thither my steps! and you, ye spirits impalpable,
Scorned by the vulgar—known to lofty souls—
Ye ghosts angelic—pure and sanctified,
And you, ye devils, visible in darkness,
Rise at my bidding! follow to the midnight stage!
                                    Exit.

Enter John Brown's Ghost.

JOHN BROWN.

Aye! follow thee we will—to hell begone,
And tell them there, "John Brown is marching
    on."   *Exit.*

SCENE V.—*Scene in Street, by Gaslight—Conger
and Baker in Dum Show—Dr. Mary Explaining
a Letter.*

BAKER.

I see nothing in that letter —nothing—
Madame Surratt could surely ask a friend
To visit her; and what more could you make of it?

DR. MARY.

True the letter, taken by itself, is nothing—
But like the occipital and ginglemns bones,
It links together high and lower parts.
You, shadow Booth, and leave his friends to me.
Herold and Atzerot have rooms adjoining his;
And I'll consult the key-hole for their secrets,
Till the vile plot comes to view.

BAKER.

Good! good! Eves-drop the villains while they
    drink,
But when they bubble over, note it down.

DR. MARY.

O, Captain, I've a glorious mission now;
Leave all to me; I'll send them up some beer,
And never plummet sank into the sea,
As I will plunge into their seething souls.

BAKER.

A good beginning! but the fox must wait,
Often to watch his chickens at the gate.
Keep to your post, and make that key-hole hear
The very whispers of their foaming beer.
                                    Exeunt.

SCENE VI.—*Atzerot and Herold Drinking—Atz-erot's Room.*

ATZEROT.

Now dot is de best beer you ever drinks.
Dot's no bottled beer, but fries from de keg—
Beer, you see, he gits flat no time atol—
De gas all fly away!

HEROLD.

Then drink before it flies.
I'm tight already; but you're a fine fellow,
And I'll do any thing in the world for you.
I'll even drink your beer.

Enter Dr. Mary Trotter.

HEROLD.

Why, Dr. Mary, as I live! Come! come!
You spinster-bottle! let me fill you up.

DR. MARY.

I hate you men; your whiskey and tobacco;
But diagnosis argues each necessity;
And my diaphragm demands some beer.

HEROLD.

The world demands that you shall have a bier.

DR. MARY.

Give me a drink.   (*Drinks.*)
My pleura argues pleurisy;
And my pneuma indicates pneumonia.
Have you read my book on bulls and horses yet?
It maps the conjugations of you men.

HERLOD.

I never read such books; they shock my piety.
Come drink again, you wormy shrimp;
There's nothing like good lager for the bots.

Offering bottle.

You bottle fly, with wings upon your hips!
No mouth, but this, would ever touch your lips.

DR. MARY.

If bottle—flies delight in carrion, I
Should drink with you, whenever I am dry.

HEROLD.

You centipede—you little rattle snake!
You pitch-fork! Do you take me for a rake?

DR. MARY.

If snakes have rattles, in their tails—egad!
Your rattles all are in your head.
If I am forkèd, so are other folk.
Then, where's the marrow of your joke?

HEROLD.

You forkèd thing! Not see it!   Why,
When meadows kiss the dusky sky,
Pitch-forks and rakes together lie.

  She boxes him, and dances out, singing Shoo-Fly.
Well, now, to business.   Where is Johnson's
   room?

ATZEROT.

Just under us, and mit de shootin—
I drops de pistol here, den runs away.

              Uncovers hole in the floor.

HEROLD.

Great God! there's Johnson in his bed!

ATZEROT.

Ya—he'sh been drunk all day—last night.
Sh! sh! sh!   *Listens and takes broom.*
Vot if she listen mit de key hole, now!
Sh! sh! sh! vait! vait!

  Slips to the door and opens suddenly—In falls
Dr. Mary.
Mine God! Vot am dot? Vot is it?
Murder! Murder! Vot is it?

              Beats Dr. Mary with a broom.

ACT III.

SCENE I.—*Theatre—Enter John Brown's Ghost, and Devils with Snakes.*

JONH BROWN.

He bade us follow, to the midnight stage—
And doing our own will, we humor his.
When first I crept into his soul at Arlington,
He trembled like an aspen; and conceived
The poison, which I smeared upon his liver,
Pregnant now,' with raw heads and bloody bones;
But as I urge him onward to the deed,
His soul recoils and plunges to and fro,
Like waters dashing to Ontario,
Just ere they reach Niagara's rock,
To clear it with an earth-quake shock!
See! see! he comes! ye waters boil;
And Hell's red serpents 'round him coil.

Enter Booth.

BOOTH.

Their costumes all in base confusion,
Like leaves of Autumn, scattered here and there,
Proclaim the last act finished, and the players
          gone.
So we who wear our bodies for the cast,
Must soon sling them down, or hang them up—
An ugly thought! and yet, a welcome one;
For every actor, whether great or small—
Whether on this stage, or the big world;
Contaminated by its loathsome fumes,
Bemoans some secret ill, and sighs for rest.
O, that I, too, could fly this fishless brook,

And meet, on yonder green celestial hill,
My kindred, and the friends of youth.
Alas! how changed, at midnight, is the stage!
Its music, actors, beauty, gone so soon—
In one short hour! Ah, yes; the stage is sad,
When those we played with, have all gone to rest!

> *John Brown holds a serpent over him.*

God! can I stand it? My brain reels!
They will not—shall not shoot Lieutenant Beall!
My very heart strings burst, and my mind wan-
    ders!
'Twill make me mad. They dare not shoot him!
Perhaps a song might soothe me. I'll try it:

> *Sings.*

"I feel like one who treads alone,
  Some banquet hall deserted,
  Whose lights are gone, whose guests are flown,
  And all but me departed."

No, it sooths me not. O, for some sweet minstrel!
Could Lilly but be here, with her sad harp—
The same she struck in yonder happy home,
For her brave brother—doomed to die so soon.
Could she but bring that wilderness of song,
This evil spirit instantly would fly,
As Merodach from Saul, when David played.

> JOHN BROWN—*Aside.*

Tell Merodach to come in here. *Laughs.*

> *Booth holds his head, as in agony, sitting.*

> BOOTH.

'Twere better far to spare the poor fool's life—
For after all, he's not the worst of men.
In sooth, he's a good man, and has a kind heart;
But good is, as good doth; and not doing well—
Gives the lie to simulation and punches
In its teeth. I'll try his goodness for a pardon;
And if he leave Lieutenant Beall to perish,

This dagger then shall probe his rottenness,
And let its filth flow, to knock men's noses up—
Tho' all the hypocrites from Hell shout murder!

Exit.

BROWN.

Still, on the dreadful brink, his soul
Recoils—too cowardly to plunge;
Next he'll be praying—then farewell
To all my conjurations. See, he comes again.

Enter Merodach—A serpent with Babboon's head.

Go Merodach and climb to his imagination—
Climb to its very heights, and coil about them,
Lashing with fiery tail, each lofty peak,
And from its pinacles, spit fire to heaven.

Enter Booth.

BOOTH.

I'll try another song, from poor Tom Moore.

Sings.

"When true hearts lie withered,
And fond ones are flown;
O, who would inhabit
This bleak world alone."

Then dearest of angels—*Kneels—Devils fly.*
No longer delay! *Angel approaches.*

Snakes run off.

Come spread your bright pinions,
And bear me away! *Rising.*
Who knows but that one single prayer
Might throw all Hell into confusion!
But was it prayer! or Tom Moore's spirit
Falling on my heart! 'Tis the poet's gift,
To weave mysterious measures for the soul;
And make calamity, a cup of consolation.
Perhaps, this was all; and yet I do feel
As though a serpent had uncoiled my heart,
And dropped back to Hell.

I'd pray again, but prayers are mere wind—
The big winds, only bump about the world;
Then why should smaller ones puff up to Heaven!
  Angels vanish and devils steal back exulting.
No—I'll wrestle with these devils all alone.
"Go tell your masters of Carroli;
That, like an eagle, in a *dove cote*,
I fluttered your volsci. *Alone I did it!*"
  Enter Conger on balcony, unseen by Booth.
Poor Lilly! when that message came to-night—
All tears and agony—she fell upon my knees,
Clung to her Prince, and bathed his robes in tears.
O, that the Prince could save him! Yes, sweet
  Lilly,
Fairest flower of the field! to die for him,
Would lead ambition to a nobler stage,
And make a tragedy to suit me well!
She reminds me of "the Last Rose of Summer"—
For other sisters blossomed in that garden then,
When Beall was radiant, as the nood-day sun,
And gave those blossoms half their beauty.
I'll sing that song for her sake.
       Sings.
"Thus kindly I scatter, thy leaves o'er the bed,
Where thy mates of the garden, lie scentless and
  dead."
By heavens! I'll scatter the leaves o'er his bed!
'Twould be a charity to send her with him,
And nothing could please the poor child better·
O, that she were nestling in this bossom now.
Drawing dagger---I'd send her sweet spirit to
  the skies,
And lay her lilly form upon his grave—
Then would I slay their enemies, and follow
  them,
To play this tragedy on some mysterious stage!

Who goes there? I saw them passing—all in
    red—
Lincoln and Johnson; Seward and his crew.
Now they climb up the masts, like monkeys—
Red jackets on them—red caps too, ha! ha! ha!
                  Clasping his head.
O, that this too billowy brain upheaving,
Would let the ships down that prance upon 't!
Their giddy masts are tickling the big clouds,
To make them laugh loud thunder, and poor
    Lincoln
Tells anecdotes to the man i' the moon.
             Conger gives great attention.
Good natured soul, I'll help him up higher.
To ride on Pegasus, or Capricon thro' Heaven.
Give us your foot boy, bounce! Alway he flies!
    ha! ha! ha!

CONGER.

Mad! Mad as a March hare!

W. BOOTH.

And now, if I know myself, the king trembled.
How he leaped down from his lofty throne,
When those players probed him to the quick.
Laughs. "How did the galled jade wince!" ha!
    ha! ha!
Yes; the rules of this most wicked world,
Tho' riding, on the heads of groaning millions,
Are tenfold weaker than a coward's knees,
While justice, even when hanging on a cross,
Can shake the universe.
But was it Hamlet, or King Lear we played?
Upon my soul, I do forget what play was acted—
Or was it Richard, shouting to the clouds,
"A horse, a horse, my kingdom for a horse!"
And was it real? or a mimic scene?
Waits the buskin, with its pompous lie?

Or was I what seemed to be—a King?
Or only Booth descended from Westminster,
Where now, in Poet's corner, sleep my fathers!
Where Shakespeare twirls his small moustache
    and smiles,
When th' elder Booth, at midnight plays again,
To Sheridan and Burke, and rare old Ben—
Moving sometimes as Brutus, on the stage,
And raising such a tempest in his wrath,
That the Ghosts all tremble, and their great kings
Run back, like mice, into their crypts.
Ha! ha! how I would like to see them run—
Those blind old mice, the Kings of England!
    ha! ha!
No, no; I am not Booth—'Twas all a dream—
And yet it must be so—for never did King Lear,
Eat oysters with Lieutenant Beall,
As I did often at Delmonico's—
Sometimes at Harvey's, on the Avenue.
And must he die so soon—he? my best friend!
The lightning rushed to tell me of his fate!
And fainted—zig-zag marks upon her cheek.

CONGER.

He needs a Doctor more than a detective.
I'll try to find his brother Edwin.

Exit.

W. BOOTH.

God! and must he stand alone!
His brave arms defiant, folded on his breast!
No, he shall have an escort. Yes, brave Prince!
King Lear is all deserted by his Court;
The tempest breaks and cracks upon his cheek—
"Only fifty attendants for a King!"
But thou shall have an escort. I will send
The whole Cabinet; who took part against me
Here to-night, with those ungrateful daughters—

Lincoln and Johnson, Seward—all; I saw them,
Laughing with those devils—black, and blue, and
    red—
Base plebeans, tricked wi' power, to mock a
    King!
Ha! ha! *Picks up Richard's crown, puts it on.*
King Lear shall wear his power again,
And his sceptre for a moment hidden thus.
                        Draws dagger.
Shall spring upon them, like the venomed snake,
Whose hissing tongue, and horny rattles shake
Such notes of war, that all the world shall quake.
                           Exit.

   *Eenter John Brown and Devils, burning brim
stone in a cauldron—all singing.*
Stir the brimstone; stir it well—
We brought it from the pits of Hell!
Stir the brimstone, let him smell
The price of bood—the stink of Hell!
Stir the brimstone, stir the snake,
We brought him from the Stygian lake.
Stir his rattles, let him shake
Such notes of war, that all the world shall quake!
        w. BOOTH, *behind scenes.*
Such notes of war, that all the world shall quake!
      JOHN BROWN, *last in procession.*
See him standing there,
The picture of despair;
How his eye balls glare!
Then, do you duty well,
And drag him down to Hell—
Drag him down, all red with blood,
Then plunge him in the Stygian flood,
And let not mercy shed a tear,
For the blood-stained murderer!

5

Enter Edwin Booth·

E. BOOTH.

Surely 'twas his voice! Wilkie, brother, speak!
No, 'twas but the loud wind, too fondly echoed,
From a brother's heart, and coined into his ac-
    cents,
Weird, unearthly sounds, that seemed to mock
    him!

Enter Baker.

E. BOOTH.

Hello, Baker! why, my brave boy,
You play the fishmonger splendidly.
But why do you detectives follow me?
You know that I am loyal.

BAKER.

Yes, that is so; we know that you are loyal,
But your brother either plays fantastic tricks
From madness, or from hatching deep designs.
Come, Booth; can you account for his strange
    conduct?

E. BOOTH.

Well, 'tis no easy matter to explain,
But listen and you'll get, at least, a glimpse.
'Tis the sad fate of actors, when o'er wrought—
Especially in tragedy—that losing the helm,
And staggering on the deck, like sailors
When a ship goes down, they drink too deeply!
Poor fellow! he can't last long at this rate.
When finishing his part to-night—his eyes
Did glow like two great balls of fire.
Even his sister stood amazed,
And his best friends fled from him.

BAKER.

But does acting make a man disloyal?
Or does it put him on the scent of blood?

E. BOOTH.

Listen, and you may partly understand:
'Tis a lonely life that actors lead—
Too often from society excluded,
Like birds of evil omen, by the sea,
They seem to meditate some tragic act;
Or more like gas-pipes, waiting for the darkness,
Their very nature takes a hue of sadness.
Their disappointments too, are manifold,
And like those other birds, that follow ships,
Players, upheld on agile wings of genius,
Diversions render to an idle crew,
For tossing them a few crumbs.
And yet in this my brother was most fortunate,
Clearing, in one year, twenty thousand dollars;
Then coining ten for one by speculation.

Enter Valco.

VALCO.

I have been to his room—he had not yet returned.

E. BOOTH—*Aside to Valco.*

Go quickly, Valco—put him on his guard—
Detectives now are on his track--
Warn him of the danger—I will hold them here.

BAKER.

Well, I must go—you can't explain him—eh?

E. BOOTH—*Taking his button-hole, confidingly.*

Stay, for a moment; I can soon explain.
Yes; he acquired suddenly a large fortune;
And yet it is the sadest thing of all,
That actors, like humming birds on flowers feed-
    ing,
Subsist upon imagination's marrow,
Whose subtle essence so can change the brain,
That truth and falsehood, in its conformation,
Play, for awhile, beau-peep—then bed together.
Conspiracies, and lusts, and stooping murder

Would thence be born, but for our pride and
    breeding—
Or to speak more properly, but for grace
Which Heaven supplies, to them who need it
    most.

        BAKER—*Pulling away.*

Well, all of that to me, Booth,
Is just about as clear as mud.

        E. BOOTH—*Clinging to his button-hole.*

Would you but listen, I could well explain him;
For th' imagination, like an angel,
Leaps from the sky, all redolent of incense,
But our perversity of will doth taint it—
And low born Lust upon his belly creeping,
Can dream of angels, and would coil them to his
    scales—
All crimes are cradled in th' imagination;
And hence the great actor playes a dangerous
    role.

        BAKER.

Damn'd if I don't believe you are all crazy.

        E. BOOTH.

To be above the common sort of men,
Is after all but Midas played upon the stage;
The Gods might turn our very brains to gold.
But who would eat them?   Do swine munch
    pearls?
Festus, or Agrippa—I forget which—
But one of them—called Saul a madman.
Now listen, for I'm coming to the point,
And will tell my brother's secret, if you'll keep it.

        BAKER.

Yes, I'll keep anything; but d—n it!
Tell me in plain language

        E. BOOTH.

I will; but recall what I have just said—

That the great actor plays a dangerous *role*;
For acting, would it move the soul, must lose
Its own conception and become reality.
'Tis a transient madness—*mikra mania*,
The Greeks believed; and when it drops the mask,
Or seems to pass away, still in the brain,
Its eggs lie buried, to hatch the *cocatrice*.
That dangerous role long hath my brother played;
Nor can you judge him, as a common man,
For he was ever Fancy's star-born child,
With agile step, to climb her flying wheels,
To snatch, with easy hand, the silken reins,
And guide her coursers thro' th' sky!

      BAKER—*Pulling away and escaping.*

I must go.   I can't understand you.   *Exit.*

      E. BOOTH—*Looking after him.*

No; and as little will this huckstering world,
The waywardness of genius, to the end of time!
Its greatest crimes, are often but misfortunes;
And its petty follies, like spots upon the sun!
And so the little things about us judge,
As children, gazing at a fire fly—
To them more splendid than a distant star—
The one, an insect—one, a glorious world—
Sometimes a world in ruins flying from its sphere
To the great mass of men a guilded rag—
Imposture finery, fading at a touch—
Or smiling sycophants flipped up to power,
Mere coin-struck images for head and tail,
Or glittering equippage for some preposterous
    fool,   .
More glorious than the majesty of mind!

                        Exit.

SCENE II.—*Street in Washington, near Madame Surratt's—Enter W. Booth Cloaked.*

W. BOOTH.

Yon weary stars, now fading one by one,
Dying, salute their Cæsar in the sky;
So these proud States, though sovereign from
      their birth,
Must yield to one great Federal power.
The very brutes have joined our brutish foes,
And seem to triumph as the stars go down;
Yon clamorous cock, impatient of the dawn,
Rings his shrill clarion to the morning air—
A proclamation to the feathered tribes,
That Federal power is armed with spurs,
And the loud clapping of his stormy wings
Shuts to the doors of mercy on his kind,
Or like some Beecher-publican, he smites
His breast, to wake yon harem from its slum-
      bers—
All covetous of light, that they may run once
      more.
Attentive to his cluck, albeit he gobbles down
The lucious worm, indifferent to their presence;
But they can gaze upon his cockish neck,
Admire his feathers glittering in the sun,
And stoop, obedient to the sultan's will!
Alas! poor States—the harem of a President!
Down, down, vile thoughts, that mix my coun-
      try's glory,
With dunghills, and the meanest of mankind,
For day is breaking, and his grey Confederate
      robe
Moves like a ghost about the Capitol.
Yon twittering birds, impatient of the chain
Which tyrant sleep had woven thro' the night,
Dart forth exulting from each parapet—

Yon revelers, returning, heel the pavements,
And echo, far away, from Arlington, replies:
O, glorious Arlington—tomb of a nation!
Thou head-board at my country's grave!
Ye marble-hearted columns, hear my vow!
My venerated sires, Virginia's sons!
And all ye great and venerable memories attest!
Enter Lilly behind, and laying her hand upon him.
Why, Lilly, you have cut my vow off just
Above its shoulders—how came you here, child?

LILLY.

Not for an instant have I slept all night,
But prayed incessantly for my poor brother;
And when I heard your voice—those silvery
    tones—
Which I depend upon to plead with Lincoln,
No longer could I keep my bed, but ran down,
To urge you forward—O, my brave friend,
Plead for his life, lose not a single moment—
Lincoln has a good heart, and you can move it.

W. BOOTH.

Just as you came, I had built up a vow;
The purport was, that should he not pardon him,
I'd strike this dagger to his heart.
          Draws dagger.

LILLY

O, terrible! May God forbid such madness!
The President is not a private citizen,
And acting in th' affairs of State, is but
A servant of the people; for his heart—
As I have just urged—is tender, and no woman
has a kinder heart than Mr. Lincoln's.
Yet Stanton and the Cabinet must be consulted;
One factor cannot cancel all, and I
Would rather see my brother perish,
By the laws of war, than that his friend

Should stoop to such a purpose!

W. BOOTH.

'Tis well for women to talk thus, but I know
All the necessities of this occasion;
And shall bear myself as Brutus, when he rose
"Refulgent from the stroke of Cæsar's fate;"
But you have not answered me—how came you
    here?

LILLY.

Madame Surratt, my friend, and this her home.
She gives her hospitality to all Confederates,
And indeed to any mortal in distress;
For her charity is boundless—how came you here?

BOOTH.

Perplexed all night, I wandered thro' the streets,
Acting sometimes King Lear, and sometimes
    Richard;
But that is past, with much quite horrible;
The dawn returns me to myself once more—
To this too real world, and your brave brother's
    fate—
Let me away to Lincoln—I'll demand his pardon.
            Flourishing a Dagger—Going.

LILLY.

O, my brave friend, use all your eloqence,
But do not harm, for my poor brother's sake.
Remember, he dies to-morrow!

W. BOOTH.

If he must die to-morrow, mark my words,
Like some great Prince, from foreign lands at
    tended,
He shall enter the courts of the Celestial King,
Followed by dignitaries, clad in purple—
Aye, in *purple* shall they stand before him!
   Flourishing Dagger--Exit--Enter Madame Surratt.

M. SURRATT.

O, my pretty Lilly, what can all this mean?
It seemed to be your voice, you pretty sinner!
And whose, dear, were those heavier silvery
    chords,
That made the night so musical?
You must come into the house, child, come, come
    in;
'Twill never do; for e'en in virtuous love,
Proprieties must be observed, or scandal,
Quick and keen as vultures on the scent,
Will pick the pupils of your reputation;
For lillies, child, are peerless in their purity;
And though their cheeks may turn up to the stars,
They dare not trust their pearly bosoms
Even to the glances of the moon.
For this St. Joseph bears them thro' the world,
While at his side the Virgin mother stands—
Then remember your name, child, come, come in,
And let me plant my lilly in her bed.

LILLY.

This mystery first to be explained.
All night long had I been praying for my brother,
When Booth, his bosom friend, came wandering
    by,
With wild soliloquies, and lured me thither.
Gone to beseige the President, he turned
Yon corner as you came.

M. SURRATT.

O, my pretty Lilly, 'tis too sad!
What can be done?   I'll go myself to Lincoln;
For well he knows me, and many favors, too,
Hath granted me—a Rebel, for her Rebel friends.
The poor, good-natured man—Heaven's blessings
    on him!
Once wept like a child, when I plead the cause

Of a deserter, whose mother was my guest.

LILLY.

A Union soldier?   His mother your guest?

M. SURRATT.

Start not, my child, for tho' this humble roof
Gives heartier welcome to Confederate friends;
Yet Union people come to me as well,
For, in the deeper sorrows of the human heart,
No party spirit ever yet could move me.
These hands would help the meanest thing that
      breathes;
My tears would always flow, perhaps too foolishly,
And some have mocked me for my childish heart,
But I would rather die the vilest death
Than spurn the poorest creature from my door.
At any rate, I plead for this deserter.
At first, when I would justify the boy,
And tried some learned precedent of law,
His Excellence put on a solemn air,
And told an anecdote, in ridicule.
At this I took another turn, and asked him thus:
Do you remember, Mr. President, your mother?
"Yes," said he, "and when I used to go to mill,
Or plowed among the daisies in the field,
I never saw a pretty flower but what
I thought of her; and when I came from school or
      work,
She always met me with her blessing, saying:
'Ab'ram, you'll one day be President!' "
I seized the cue, and, aiming quick, exclaimed:
Suppose that mother, kneeling at your feet,
      should say:
"Spare the poor boy; O, spare him for his
      mother's sake!"
At this I paused.   The magistrate seemed strug-
      gling
With his filial heart.   The strong man trembled

And I added: "Could you spurn your mother
From your feet? I am a mother, too, and know
A mother's heart!" At this the tears rushed down
His rugged face, and rising hastily, he said,
Placing meanwhile his hand upon his heart:
"Go tell his mother, madam, that my mother
Pleads for the boy—that I have pardoned him."

LILLY--*Clasping Madame Surratt.*

O, madam, we have a loving mother, too:
Go plead for her—for me—for all of us,
And save my brother if you can.

MADAME SURRATT.

Hark! hark! 'tis th' angels! now angels sing,
And I have learned thro' life, that God most honors
Th' enterprise that early honors Him.
'Tis th' angels of St. Dominic. That island,
Once a den of thieves, has risen thro' this Saint,
And thro' the sweet lives of his hooded monks,
To eminence in all good works—see, see!
With misty caps upon their venerable heads,
Yon hills of Maryland salute the morn;
Let us salu e the real sun, of whom
Yon fiery orb is but a passing shade.
Perhaps the shadow of his crown—wee'll first.
Prefer our suit before the King of Kings!

LILLY.

Stay, stay! my rosary yet in bed,
Keeps company with tears upon it shed,
Where all night long I counted, one by one,
Those bloody drops in mem'ry of God's Son,
And paid to every bead a tear—ah, me!
From Bethlehem to Calvary!
Then wait one moment till my rosary brings
Its mournful tribute to the King of Kings!

Exit.

O, charming child! those beads, me thinks, in
    Heaven,
Will plead upon thy cheek, O, thou Immaculate!
Then Lincoln cannot halt, for thou didst give
Thy precious tears to mingle in the font,
Which brought him to the gate of Paradise—
That font was water, and that water blood—
Gushing for all mankind!
What tho' ambition, shattered his pure faith.
Still from its crevices do flowers spring,
And o'er the desert waste an influence fling.
He loves his mother, and her God-like faith;
It must come back to him, thro' life and death,
Nor can he spurn us, when we plead for one.
Baptized with him—our Holy Mother's son!

    *Enter Annie Surratt, who runs to her mother
and kisses her.*

ANNIE.

Kiss me again, sweet mother dear, O, mother,
Such a dream as I had last night!
'Twas but a dream, but O, so terrible!
Me thought some soldiers dragged you to a cell,
Where vermin crawl'd about your precious form,
And all the while they mocked you for your faith,
Then loaded you with chains, and then, O, God!
A dismal scaffold rose up to my view,
To which you tottered with a crucifix,
Oft kissing it and bathing with your tears.
Good Father Walters, too, was at your side,
Sustained your tottering step and comfort gave;
I shrieked and woke—kiss me again, sweet
    mother!

MRS. SURRATT.

Our stomachs, over-gorged, may night-mares breed

More numerous than the mares of Thessaly;
Yet dreams, my child, do sometimes come to
    pass;
Prophets and priests have often been forewarned
While dreams ran up and down on Jacob's
    ladder—
Warned by a dream, St. Joseph took the child
And fled with him to Egypt, that same land
Where Joseph plucked from Pharoa's mystic
    dream
The coming corn, to stay the direful famine.

ANNIE.

Ah, yes; and in that very dream, to Joseph given,
A gibbet rose to view, such as I saw.

MADAME SURRATT

The very mornings of this world are sad,
And come to us, each day, subdued by tears,
As a sweet mother gazing on her prodigals.
The very crosses on our foreheads, child,
Draw blood—and hence these ashes to remind
    us—
Traced by our mother church—Ash Wednesday.
What wonder, then, if you and I should suffer?
Sufferings must come, but dreams can never
    bring them.

ANNIE.

O, mother, what I saw was real;
No language could express it—it was real.

MADAME SURRATT.

More dreams, my child, than moons have been
    fulfilled;
But prophets only—such as Joseph was—
Can pluck the beard of coming Time, ere yet
The morning wets it with her tears, or hold
Him to account, while in the bosom of his God.
Cheer up—forget it all—'twas but a dream—

6

Some fairy fancy tickling with a straw,
And playing on the tendrils of your heart!
Why do you weep—ha! ha! ha!—you little goose?
Go, get your wrapping; we are late for Mass.

ANNIE—*Going, returns.*

One moment more; I had another dream;
I thought that Lilly, pale and sad,
Stood moaning by the sea with J. Wilkes Booth.
Some soldiers fired, and her brother fell.
Booth clasped her in his arms, and all was silent;
Silent as death—the very air stood still.
Then a ghost rose—her brother's ghost.
Ah, me! it was a horrid sight—most horrible!

Exit.

MADAME SURRATT.

How strange!   'Tis more than strange!   'Tis
    wonderful!
For Lilly's history—to her unknown—
Her brother's, too—it seems prophetical.
The very winds are ever full of prophecies,
And God asserts himself in every breeze,
As well as in the thunder storm;
But most of all, doth He delight to dwell
In human hearts by suffering sanctified!
Then give me sufferings and make this heart
An humble palace for the Prince of Peace!

Enter John Surratt, excited.

JOHN SURRATT.

Well, mother, I have the whole plot complete.

MADAME SURRATT.

Plot?

JOHN SURRATT.

Yes, plot; no plot in the grave-yard mother;
No plot to burn the Capitol; no villainy;
But simply, (if you please to call it so,)
A purpose, and a good one, too—a plan

To seize the President and take him South.

MADAME SURRATT.

Oh! oh! for Heaven's sake, my son, desist;
'Twould cost your life. O, listen to your mother!

JOHN SURRATT.

'Twas ever thus. "Oh!" "oh!" "aw!" "aw!"
    whenever
Fortune beckons me, and bids me move,
You interpose. "Aw!" "oh!"what splendid reason-
    ing!
Then, not convincing me, you run to church,
And thwart me by your prayers—they always
    balk me,
Drive me back, and turn my hopes to ashes!

MADAME SURRATT.

Well, son, your mother may be a great fool;
But fools can sometimes give advice,
And if ever my prayers prevailed in Heaven,
To thwart your purpose, Heaven is foolish, too.

JOHN SURRATT.

I don't mean that.   Our plan is simply this:
To seize the President, but not to harm him;
To take him prisoner of war and save the South.
All has been arranged, and I must do my part,
But promise you this, mother, to shed no blood.
To seize the President and keep him safe;
And this I will do, cost what it may.

Exit.

MADAME SURRATT.

A woman's reasoning, fruitless as her tears!
But not so vain, a weeping mother's prayers—
They must prevail, for God hath wedded here,
(*Hand on her heart,*) Eternal sentiments of love
    and prayer.
A mother's love, a mother's prayers were given,

To plead, like angels, at the Gate of Heaven!

Exit.

Enter Annie, Lilly following her from the stage.

SCENE III.—*President's Mansion—Lincoln alone,*
Reading alone.

LINCOLN.

I would rather split rails in Illinois
For fifty cents a day than run this Government;
For who can tell, in these great waves of State,
As bran new questions press him to the chin,
Where the next step might sink him?
Now, when I practiced law out West,
The judge and jury always took a part;
But here, as President, I stand alone;
For Cabinets and councellors are nothing.
Great causes were entrusted to me then—
Partly because I knew some law; but more,
(As country people often have expressed it,)
Because "old Abe could never be bought off."
But there's one bribe, and only one, that tempts
     me—
That's when a poor mother pleads with her tears;
For when I read the wrinkles of her face,
That book of books, telling its mournful tale,
My own dear mother rises from the ground.
By Heavens! She always turns me to a baby.
I was her first and only child, and do believe
I'll be a baby to the last! My mother's booby!
A President should be made of better grit;
And I was never fit for such an office.

Enter Page.

PAGE.

That fisherman, your Excellence, whom
You saw last evening.

LINCOLN.

Bring him in.

Enter Baker.

BAKER.

Our office, please your Excellence, is delicate,
And you have charged us never to arrest
In doubtful cases.   Now, one of your friends—
Whom we have often seen in these apartments—
Is either crazy or your direst foe.
We found him in the streets last night; a dagger
Of't he brandished in the air, and cursed you
    bitterly.
'Twas Booth, the actor, coming now to see you,
And I hastened up to put you on your guard.

LINCOLN.

O, don't mind him. He was only acting tragedy.
True, he's a Rebel, for he tells me so;
But men who talk loudly are never dangerous.
Now, when a Rebel tries to lead the crowd,
I slap the law upon him quick as lightning;
And that's the way I snatched Vallandingham;
But men like Booth—mere talkers—do no harm.
My motto from the first has been,
"Malice to none, but charity for all."

BAKER.

Well, your Excellence, I've nothing more to say.
                                          Exit.

LINCOLN.

Well, certain, it is that I have done my best.
In cases of doubt, I lean to mercy's side,
That, when I come to die, mercy may lean to me;
But when I know the law, laid down in prece-
    dent,
Or growing up from roots of truth and justice,
I'll execute it certain as a gun!
                                    Reading.
Now here's a bran new case—Lieutenant Beall's.
Captured with letters of marque and reprisal,

He claims that they protect him in our lines,
But whether such letters hold on the lakes—
(Even if our lakes are great inland seas,)
As well as on the ocean—"*that is the question.*"
If on the lakes, then on the rivers, too;
If on the rivers, then within our lines;
And so a spy—covered up by fools' cap—
Might claim exemption and demand exchange.

Enter Booth—Lincoln shakes hands.

Why, Booth, can you afford to play all night,
And then get up before the chickens?

BOOTH.

Thus early do I come, your Excellence,
To plead for justice and Lieutenant Beall.
Glow-worms are not so plentiful of late,
And he who hopes to find them, must rise early.
Resplendent do they sparkle on the robes of
        night,
But hide their radience from the garish day;
So justice shines, perhaps, in other lands;
But in this land of light 'tis rarely found.
Preachers are plentiful, and piety a drug;
But even-handed justice, where is she?
Scarcer than glow worms, muffling up their
        faces!
Or, since you speak of chickens—"scarcer than
        hens' teeth;"
And yet she sometimes springs forth like a ser-
        pent.

Clutching his dagger.

Th' avenging Nemesis may be at hand.
Rome had a Brutus—England a Cronwell—
Mark my words.

LINCOLN—*Exposing his bosom*
Well, Booth, that reminds me of a coon-hunt

That I once had in Illinois.   Jim Douglas—
Cousin, you know, to Stephe Douglas—not Fred;
O, no, not Fred; I never hunt with him—
He clomb a tree, where we had treed the coon,
And crawled out on a limb to catch him.
What did the coon do, but make a dash at
    Douglas.
Under the limb he went, and the coon passed--
As Jim would say when he played poker.
Now, cypress limbs, you know, are very slick,
And Jim could never get on top again.
He tried hard to chin it--full thirty feet
Above the ground, ha! ha! ha!—and giving up at
    last, cried out:
"Hold the dogs, Abe, for God's sake hold the
    dogs!"
But could I hold some twenty dogs or more?
So down he fell, and the dogs piled on him, ha!
    ha! ha!
Now, Booth, if I should pardon everybody,
The dogs would pile on me. But there's no coon
That ever scared me yet.   I'll keep on top o' the
    limb.

Exposing his bosom.

BOOTH.

O, the hard-hearted villain!   One argument—
Clutches dagger.

And only one can reach him;
But that must be the last!

To Lincoln.

Letters of marque and reprisal should protect
    him,
And, in the name of justice, I demand his pardon!

LINCOLN.

'Pon my word I'm sorry for the young man;

But Booth, you don't know what I have to con-
    tend with,
Nor my responsibilities.

        BOOTH—*Clutching dagger.*
Then I suppose he dies to-morrow.

        LINCOLN—*Exposing his bosom.*
Yes; for in my heart—true to this great country,
I can find no place for pardon.

        BOOTH—*Aside.*
I'll try once more.
What if you yourself were on the scaffold,
Condemned unjustly to a cruel death—
Suppose—

        LINCOLN.
The fact is, if the sentence was unjust—
And I could see it, in that light, I'd pardon him—
But, as you say in Hamlet—"*that is the question.*"

        BOOTH.
Hear me once more.   When I was playing Rich-
    elieu,
You swore that I had taught you statesmanship;
And when I played Piscara the Apostate,
You promised me whatever I might ask.
Beall is my bosom friend, and has a sister,
Weeping—praying—almost dying of her grief,
He stands between us, hinged upon this breast,
And like the lintel of some fair palace door,
She meets him ever, and her kisses bring—

        LINCOLN—*Interrupting him.*
That kind of talk Booth, always reminds me
Of a small ear of corn, in a big shuck;
And if you, expect my lip to hang down, like it,
Then you mistake the stalk.
Old Davy Crocket was the man for me.
His motto was:

"Be sure you're right, then go ahead."
I'll tell you an anecdote about old Davy:
'Twas said, you know, that he could grin a coon
    down
From the tallest tree in wild cat bottom;
So, another chap, he tried to cry one down,
But he did'nt.   Now, I'm like those coons,
As long as I do right, they can't cry me down,
No, nor grin me down neither.   They may make
    faces;
Call me babboon; old fool, or what they please;
But, as my old mother used to say;
Abram *do right*, and the whole world can't hurt
    you!
But Booth, as I said before—if I knew
The sentence to be unjust, I'd pardon him.

BOOTH—Scornfully.

If you knew the sentence to be unjust?
Rather say, if I did know it to be just,
Then would I summons? every man-of-war,
And every monitor that rides the wave—
That they should thunder to the clouds,
And shake this continent, or save him!
Scornfully—"If you knew the sentence to be un
    just!"
Then know another sentence to be just!

Advances towards him with dagger clutched.

And learn that nature, sovereign from her birth,
And all her children, sovereign from their birth,
Disdain and spit upon an unjust government—
With thunder hath she clad the patriot's arm,
And mine—*Advancing.*

Enter little Tad, kissing his father.

TAD.

O, Papa, I had a dreadful dream last night!
'Twas awful, awful!   O, 'twas awful!

BOOTH—*Aside.*

Angels and Saints, do walk about this world,
And take ten thousand forms, to shape our lives!
Men are but children, children in disguise—
We need our nurses, till we reach the skies.

Exit.

Enter Madame Surratt and Lilly.

MADAME SURRATT.

Behold the sister of Lieutenant Beall,
Condemned, your Excellence, to die to-morrow.
His poor old mother, too, is on her knees,
Imploring Heaven, to bless your Excellence,
And spare her boy.

LILLY—*Kneeling.*

O, spare my brother, good kind, sir.
O, spare him for his mother's sake;
For mine! O, spare him! spare him!

LINCOLN—*Aside.*

The very name of mother makes a child of me.

Wiping his eyes.

And I hate to look like a fool.
Ladies you must excuse me for a moment.
I'll eh!— I'll eh!—

Madame Surratt falls at his feet.

MADAME SURRATT.

Behold in me, good sir, the poor boy's mother—
Your mother, too, will bless you from the skies!

LILLY.

Pray don't leave us—say, good sir;
Say, will you pardon him!—do kind sir,
For me—my mother's—your mother's sake!

LINCOLN.

I will—I pardon him—go tell his mother.

LILLY.

Thanks! thanks! ten thousand thanks! May
Heaven bless your Eexcellence!

LINCOLN.

Go child, and be a good girl, for women—
Say what you will about their weaknesses,
Do leave, in sending out great armies to the
    world,
A something, in the heart of every man,
To which, as Boatmen say out West!
"'*Twill do to tie to!*" ha! ha! ha!   *Aside.*
And they know damned well how to fix the
    ropes! ha! ha!

To Ladies

Now go home, and use your power with discre-
    tion;
For power you have, although you may not
    know it.
Yes; every home is but a miniature of State,
And woman there, tho' dressed in home-spun
    checks,
Is God's own Angel, sent to guard the gate.
Ah, yes; I know, and well remember one—
My mother—more than all the world to me—
And tho' her destiny was obscure,
Her grave forgot—without a stone to mark
That lowly bed —yet still she rules the State—
Great armies do her bidding; and her mercy
Falls to-day, on you, my child!
But ladies you'll excuse me now;
For I must write the pardon.

    Exeunt, except Lincoln— Writes the pardon.

Yes; woman's mission is indeed sublime,
Tho' self-approving man may thumb his pits,
And ape the peacock, when he spreads his tail,
Yet woman, less obtrusive, guides his feet;
For woman, at the cradle, rocks the world;
And plants, with every lullaby, some germ,
To ripen for the future man—his plow

To guide, to rule the Senate by his tongue,
Or plant on flaming battlements, his banner;
'Tis her's to teach, in every sphere—her tears
Have won great battles, and her frown subdued
The mightiest Kings—while more than these:
Her smile lights up the ruins of a fallen world;
Her prayers, more potent still, can burst
The gates of Heaven, and climb the throne of
    God!
Patient in grief—in fortitude sublime.
When man becomes the weaker vessel and de-
    spairs,
She hooks him, from the billow, with her faith,
Puts back his drowning locks, and points him to
    the stars!

                  Enter Seward.

Seward I wish I was out of this business.
I'd rather plow, split rails, or keep a doggery—
Anything, by Heaven! is better than President.
Jeff Davis and his crew, keep up this fight,
But I'd make peace to-morrow if could.

            SEWARD.

Would you allow secession, Mr. President?

            LINCOLN.

No; I don't mean that—I'd sink every ship
That floats our flag upon the waves—
Bury our last army with its banners,
And then go down into the gulf myself,
Or save this Union!

            SEWARD.

What then is the trouble.

            LINCOLN.

These women bother me—sisters and mothers.
By Heavens! Seward, I can't see a woman cry.
Your heart is cold as ice; but mine wilts
Whenever I see a mother in distress,

They have all been pleading here for that young
    Beall,
And I have pardoned him.

             SEWARD.

Impossible! You cannot—*must not* pardon him.

             LINCOLN.

                  Handing pardon.

Well, there 't is—I have pardoned him already.
Give it to Stanton—he will send it forward,
I take the responsibility.

                        Exit.

             SEWARD.

I, too, will take responsibility.
Your woman's heart would rend this Union thus.

                Tears up the pardon.
                Enter Wilkes Booth.

             BOOTH.

I come to thank his Excellence and you
For your gracious pardon of Lieutenant Beall.
It brings me back, once more, to happier
    thoughts,
And stifles in my heart, a dreadful purpose;
For this one act of justice to my friend,
Presages justice to my native land.
Upon my soul, I thank ye both most heartily!

             SEWARD.

The pardon is revoked—I would not have it—
And the felon dies to-morrow.

             BOOTH.

Villain, you lie!   He is no felon.

       Seizes Seward—Shaking him violently.

But a soldier, every inch—thou the felon—
Your own sons felons, to be dragged, ere long,
Before their country's bar for peculation—
That George your model thief, and Fred

7

Spawned from the same serpent.   O, I would
        tear you
Limb from limb, to save my suffering friend—
A man—a soldier—-born to be your master—
Cold hearted villain go!

Hurls him off
Exeunt.

ACT IV.

SCENE I.—*Scene near the Fort on Governor's Island—New York—Night—Thunder and Lightning—Enter* BOOTH.

Mysterious powers! whose lightning spurs drive
    on
Th' unsaddled winds—whose plumes of light
    touch Heaven,
But vanish ere our tongues can bid ye halt!
If ever ye to mortals, in distress, stoop down—
To shipwrecked mariner, or to hearts more
    wrecked,
To bring them Heaven's pitying love, or cove-
    nants,
From Hell, to make a compact for their souls;
Behold, in me, your vassal thro' all time,
For this one benison—to burst yon gates,
And guide me to the dungeon of my friend.

             Enter John Brown's ghost.
          BROWN.

That's a bargain; give us your bone, old boy ;
Don't try that gate, but come along with me.
I know a sentinel—a poor, soft fool—
In love with a girl down South, just talk your
    nonsence,
For awhile to him, and he'll let you pass;
But Yanks, you know, mean business when they
    trade.
Then swear, by every sacred thing in Heaven,
To ratify this bargain for your soul.

BOOTH.

Aye, Heaven and earth I barter—lead me on!

Excunt.

SCENE II.—*Sentinel pacing at door of prison.*

SENTINEL.

Halt.   *Enter Booth.*

BOOTH.

Soldier, I have a friend imprisoned here;
He dies to-morrow, and I come to bear
His dying message to his home.

SOLDIER.

My orders are most positive—you cannot.

BOOTH—*Giving pocketbook.*

Then this is yours—'tis all I have on earth;
Checks, well endorsed, and on your greatest
        banks.
'Twill make you rich and bless your friends!

SOLDIER.

No; not for all the money in New York.

BOOTH.

Soldier, were you once dandled on a father's
        knee?
Perhaps a sister graced your happy home.
My friend's poor sister, now, by yonder wave,
Is weeping, praying, dying of of her grief;
And you will let me pass to speak one word.

SOLDIER.

My orders are most positive—you cannot.

BOOTH.

Soldier, have you a mother, brother, child?
Hast any friend or home, wife or betrothed,
To whom your soul, in death, would turn?

SOLDIER.

Nor wife, nor children, scarce a friend on earth;
Perhaps one heart, but only one, regards me.
That one far away, and in the ruined South.
My poor mother pined away and died,

When I was wounded at Manassas Junction,
Or rather died embracing me when I returned;
And never, while life lasts, can I forget
A Rebel enemy, who passed me through their
    lines,
T'embrace that mother on the bed of death.

BOOTH.

Behold in me a pilgrim from that land,
Whose generous son was thus your friend!
Dying, you say, she pressed you to her heart!
To that some breast on which your cheek re-
    clined,
Dimpled and painted by the life she gave.
Soldier, suppose that you were doomed to die,
And that a comrade came the night before,
To bear your dying message to that mother;
Take this with all—a fortune in your grasp!

SOLDIER.

Take back your purse—I would not have it—
    pass.
This very night the watch-word is "Manassas!"
                                    Walks off.

BOOTH.

O, generous nature, thou didst urge my prayer;
And rugged hearts, whose adamantine walls
Had scorned the thunder from a thousand battle-
    ments,
Grow weak as infancy at thy sweet voice!
                                    Exit.

SCENE III.--Beall's Prison—Beall Sleeping—
            Enter Booth.

O, generous nature, here we meet again,

For thou dost soothe and hold him to thy heart;
Sweet mother of us all, keep horrid dreams,

And the dread to come, far from his lonely pillow;
O, nerve him for the conflict; and his soul,
Cast in thy noblest and most generous mould,
O, gently lead it to the sacrifice!
No flowers to deck the victim's brow; but fame
Shall hang her golden locks about his temples,
While beauty, far away, in Southern clime,
Shall render tears unbidden, to his name;
And e'en the generous foeman shall exclaim,
"Alas! for so much manly beauty lost—
"Such bravery and worth to perish in the storm!"
See! see! he smiles.

BEAL.

Laughing in sleep.

Run, children, run to the other side.
Come, Lilly, let me see—O, you little rogue,
You've slipped the bandage from your eye.

Laughs.

BOOTH.

'Tis blind-man's buff. He plays it with his sister,
And dreams have borne him back to childhood's
      shore.
How strangely do they mix our lives!
Now roses mount upon his pallid cheek,
Like flowers that hang upon a precipice,
Unconscious of the gulf beneath.   See! see!

Beall starts and trembles.

Some great o'er mastering thought convulses
      him—
Perhaps the gibbet rises to his view—
I'll call him from the dreadful dream.

BEAL.

Run, children, run, th' Indians are coming down.
I see Tecumsie, with ten thousand braves;
O, run, my pretty Lilly—run! run! run!
I'll hold them back until you reach the barn!

Back! back! you painted villains—back, I say!
Springing from his couch, grappling for his sword.
Where! Where is my sword?

BOOTH.

Your sword, brave boy, surrendered to the foe,
Now leaves you quite defenseless—take this
    dagger!

Throws cloak over him.

BEALL.

Why, Booth! how came you here?

Embracing him.

BOOTH.

I come to take your place—have won the guard.
The pass-word is "Manassas"—take this dagger,
    fly—
For I would kiss the bony cheeks of death,
To give you back once more to life and liberty.

BEALL.

Et tu Brute! And has it come to this?
Am I so poor—so fallen in your esteem!
What, skulk from death, and leave my friend to
    die?

BOOTH.

Forgive me—no—'tis only for a moment—fly!
Go meet your sister, weeping in yon cove,
Close to the rock, and nearest to the wave.
Be quick, and go, for you can soon return;
Her lantern rocks on yonder dancing boat,
To guide your feet and beckons you to come.

BEALL.

Ten thousand thanks, my good, brave friend!
That will I do—keep ward 'till my return,
And prove yourself a soldier at my post.
Once more liberty—to the fresh air and skies,
To thee sweet Lilly, for one parting word!

One message to my home, then all farewell!

BOOTH.

The last of Paradise for him on earth!
'Twas a great folly so to wound his soul,
And yet, to take his place and bid them fire,
Had been ambition's loftiest pinacle—
My heart's supreme delight.   But let it pass,
The future still is mine, and they shall know it,
For I will strike them in their lecherous beds,
Or midst their revelries and pleasures smiling;
With all their sins full cankered to the green;
To start a wrinkle on the nose of Hell!

SCENE IV.—*On Sea shore—Lilly with Lantern
by a Shed, and Great Rocks—Boat Anchored.*

LILLY.

O, I do tremble so!   Perhaps those signs
In Heaven and earth, which fright the chirping
      birds,
And moaning beasts, just ere an earthquake's
      shock
Are given to human souls, before calamity!
But let it come, earthquake tempest, I
Have cast, in Heaven, the anchor of my bark--
In Heaven shall find it opened to a cross,
There twined wi' flowers, and brighter than the
      sun!
Yet, O, he was so brave and manly beautiful!
So far above the common-sort of men;
That when he passed, all hearts did give him
      reverence;
Such gentleness and power in concert joined,
Such majesty in one exalted mind—
He seemed an angel, stooping to mankind!

Heavens! joy! joy!—but do I dream?—'tis he 'tis
    he!

Enter Lieutenant Beall—Flys to his arms, weep-
ing.

But, how is this? Your pardon was revoked!

                     Kisses her.

BEALL.

Alas! no pardon granted me. I come,
Paroled in honor, by a generous friend,
To send a parting message to our home,
And first to her, my mother, O, my mother!
Kiss me again! Tell her that I died a soldier.
O, tell her, for her bruised heart's consolation,
That, with all my waywardness, no mortal sin
Was left unshriven on my parting soul;
That never did I shed one drop of blood,
But in the fair and open field of war.
To my superiors have obedient been,
And condescending to the poorest soldier;
To prisoners, in my power, was always kind—
More gentle to the fallen foe, than friends;
Surrendered when no valor could avail,
And died, at last, as she would have me die!

            Taking locket from his neck.

This, give to her whose precious name it bears,
And say that I will wear her image in my soul.

            Kisses her, parting.

Farewell forever, love.   *Lilly swoons.*
Farewell! Farewell!

                Exit.

LILLY.

                Recovering.

Gone, gone; O, never to return; gone, gone!
Ye Heavens, let your loudest thunders peal!
In thunders, O, ye saints—thou queen of Heaven,

O, plead with God, that He may strike them
    down—
Plead that yon sun may never rise again,
Too glorious signal for a deed so foul!
Let darkness swallow Heaven and earth;
While Calvary groans again, and angels weep!

Kneels.
Enter Booth.

BOOTH.

Come, Lilly, we must hasten from this place.

LILLY.

In such an hour as this. I dare not stir.
Down! Down upon your knees!!

BOOTH.

Your brother sends, by me, his last request;
'Tis that you hasten from this place.

LILLY.

O, tell me his sweet words—speak them again.

BOOTH.

Aside.

Should she remain and hear the signal gun,
'Twould drive her to madness. Let me try once
    more!

To Lilly

My life is now at stake, and we must fly;
The baited dogs are on my track—come, come!

*Seizes her hand, when she snatches away, and
runs up the rocks.*

LILLY.

See, see, the sun is rising!

*Covers her Eyes—Dead March in the Distance—
Long Silence—Signal Gun Fires—Booth Supports
Her—Beall's Ghost in Confederate Uniform—
Blood on His Face.*

LILLY, *as Ophelia.*

I knew that you would come to me again,

You pretty bloodhound! Come, come, catch
    the fox!
Foxes have holes, and birds have nests—ha!
    ha! ha!
And we poor Southern birds—come, let's fly.
The mocking-birds await us, and magnolias throw
Their censers up to Heaven—ha! ha! ha!
Those grand old priests, in Temples of the Sun!
Come, come, my love, go home! go home! go
    home!
        Weeps—Kneels to Beall—Booth Weeping.
Don't stay from mama, boy; home! home! home!

SCENE V. —*Confederate   Camp—Moonlight—*
    Enter Beall's Ghost.

GHOST.

Once more my spirit walks Virginia's hills,
Once more thy voices, O, my native land—
More musical than waves, and winds salute me!
Ye warblers of the night—sweet mocking-birds,
Long had I lost your melodies, unknown,
To yonder frozen clime; but now me meet again;
Ye whippoorwills—my childhood's wonder, hail!
Sing on, O, sing a requiem to the past.
Hail, hail, Confederate camp! Ye heroes hail!
My tentless comrades, sleeping on the ground;
Undaunted Lee! a falling nation's pride!
Confederate arms, still gleaming unsubdued,
My native land—ye hills and mountains hail!
                  Exit.
      Enter lame Confederate Sentinel.

SENTINEL.

I'd rather fight all day than keep this watch;
What if I fall asleep, they could but shoot me.
No, by Jupiter, I'll be a soldier to the last;

But my wound pains me; let me ride this log.

Straddles a log.

Who goes there! Halt! halt!

VOICE.

Hello, Johnny Reb, will you give me some tobacco for a drink?

SENTINEL.

Yes, if you'll toat fair—come in.

Enter Union scout.

SCOUT.

Do you fellows get anything to eat down here?

SENTINEL.

Yes, plenty of it—where's your whisky?

SCOUT.

Here.

Gives canteen and sentinel drinks.

SENTINEL.

That's what old Stonewall used to take from Banks.

Here's your tobacco.

Gives it.
Drinks agian.

Now go.

SCOUT.

Going.

And you go to sleep, you damned old Reb.

SENTINEL.

Hold on- what's your hurry?

SCOUT.

I have to travel twenty miles before daylight. Good-night, good-night.

SENTINEL.

Drinks again.

By Jupiter, he's a good soldier;
That's the kind of powder I like to smell.

Smells.

It makes me feel good all over—ha! ha! ha!

Drinks—business—Stretches out and sleeps.
Enter ghost of Beall.

GHOST.

O, that this hollow tree of spirit life
Could put once more its antlered branches on,
Then would I make them knock at Heaven's
    gate—
To call sweet mercy down to my poor sister.
How did she flutter, like a bird upon the ground,
Smit by the gun that told my doom.

Exit.
Enter Captain Powel.

POWEL.

What, soldier, sleeping at your post?

SENTINEL.

Staggering.

Why, Captain Powel—Thornton Powel—yes.
Well, Cap., you see how it is—my leg hurts me;
I was wounded, you know, at Fredericksburg,
And it got so stiff that I had to lie down.

POWEL.

Your legs both seem limber enough now.

SENTINEL.

Now, none of your game—now Cap—now
    Thornton—
Thor—Thor—Thornton Powel, I'm your friend,
And if you have me shot, ha! ha! ha!
You'll disgrace our family.   Ha! ha! ha!

POWEL.

You're too brave a soldier to be shot;
Go, I'll not report you—go back to camp,
And let me take your watch.

S

SENTINEL.

Going.

That's all right, ha! ha! ha! O, you're the soldier
   tor me.

Exit.

Staggers back.

Let me tell you, captain; either I saw
Lieutenant Beall to-night, or drempt it.
He came up in Confederate grey, a rope
Around his neck, and talked about his sister.
Cap., I do believe he was drunk—ha! ha! ha!
Dream, or reality—it makes me skittish—ha!
   ha! ha!

Whistles—Looks down road—Exit.

Damn'd if I'm afraid of ghosts.

Whistles Dixie

POWEL.

Alas! it might be true, for he was captured,
And the villains may have shot him,
Hanged him for aught, we know—infernal
   thieves!
But, as the world goes now a days, 'tis questioned,
Whether they who live, or they who die, are
   happiest.

Re-enter drunken soldier.

POWEL.

Go, go to camp!

SENTINEL.

Well, Cap., I came back to tell you—now, Cap.;
I'm not so drunk, for down in yonder shade,
In the white blossoms of a dog-wood tree,
That same grey form appeared; and more than
   that—
A Yankee scout was here to-night,
And I came back to put you on your guard.
The villain might be prowling for your scalp.

Good-night—O, I am not afraid of ghosts!

Whistles and staggers off.

Exit.

POWEL.

The full, round orb of yon descending moon,
Looks down upon the grave of Stonewall
  Jackson;
Perhaps the grave of these Confederate States—
Hark, the sad notes of the lonely whippoorwill!
Like some sweet poet of the sunny South,
He flings himself desparing on the ground,
To sing thy requiem. O, my native land!
The very air seems heavy, and I sometimes think
That we mysterious mortals leap the wall,
Reared by a jealous future, 'gainst our noses.
For aught I know, the universe itself,
All peopled and piled up, looks down upon us,
As does the audience of a great theater,
Which tears out one wall from every edifice,
To peep in on our most domestic scenes.
For aught I know, spirits might robe themselves,
When great events come trooping on the heels
  of time.
Who goes there! Halt! halt! 'Twas like a man,
Yet vanished in an instant; and, by Heaven!
'Twas very like some one whom I have seen!
"In such a place, in such an hour as this,
"Descending spirits have conversed with men,
"And told the secrets of the dread unknown."
See! see! It comes again—halt, soldier, halt!
But one step more, and on thy peril—halt!

Ghost waives him back.

It halts, but seems to motion with its hand,
As tho' 'twould bid me hold my fire—then speak!

Ghost advances.

What e're thou art—if sentinel or spy—

Whether messenger from Heaven or Hell—
What e're thy mission -spy or Devil—halt!

Fires.

Yet, there it stands—stone still—struck by my
    ball.
For blood comes oozing from its grey Confed-
    erate coat—
Blotches of blood on that familiar face!
Would God I had not fired—speak, soldier—
    speak!

GHOST.

When nations fall, their crash wakes up the dead;
And I have left my grave for a short term,
To walk my native hills, and on the crumbling
    edge
Of these Confederate States—a crater vast—
Would point you to a gulf most horrible.
E're yet yon moon proclaim the paschal feast,
And on the day that Christ was crucified,
The powers of Hell shall blacken all this land;
For dignitaries great shall roll in blood,
While Ruin drives her ebon car abroad,
Not womanhood nor helpless age,
Nor infancy can walk this world secure.
But e're that hour, I come to ask one boon—
The friendship of a soldier for a soldier's sister.

POWEL.

What e'er thou wilt; my life is in thy hand;
But tell me, thou impalpable, august—
And most mysterious thing; say, what thy name?
And what the great event you prophesy?
What dignataries, they to roll in blood,
My friends or foes?

GHOST.

Both friends and foes, commingling in the storm.
Shall fly like leaves of Autumn to yon gulf,

And leave both Federal and Confederate States
Beheaded, and their trunks, a gory mass
Thrown at the foot of Calvary on that day
Which saw the crucifixion—ask no more.

POWEL.

But tell me, who art thou? and who thy sister?

GHOST.

I was thy comrade—once Lieutenant Beall;
But now his helpless Ghost, without my sword;
Or I would strike and strike them to the last—
Disarmed, defenceless, prisoner of war,
Hanged in cold blood, in hearing of my sister,
Who by the signal gun was so afflicted,
That reason tottered from its throne—her mind,
That fairest palace of the world, fell down—
And now a maniac, lost and wretched in her
    woe,
She seeks my grave, and often calls for you.
Go friend, console her, if you can, and Heaven
May graciously restore the farest flower,
That ever offered insence to the skies.
Farewell! farewell!

PAYNE.

Stay, stay. Where shall I find her? Speak!

GHOST.

Go to the tomb of Washington. His Grave
She decks with flowers, and bids him make
A little room for me. Farewell! farewell!

POWEL.

Then all is lost!
My home—my love—my country gone!
Heaven and Earth farewell!

Enter Sentinel.

SENTINEL.

What, soldier; no watch word?
You're a pretty sentinel.

POWEL.

Stand to your watch soldier—good night—good
   night!

SENTINEL

But I heard a gun fire hereabouts.

POWEL.

'Twas I that fired—good night—good night!

SENTINEL.

But stay.   What was it?   Why did you fire?

POWEL.

'Twas very strange, a most prodigious thing—
'Twas monstrous—most astonishing—good
   night!

Exit.

SENTINEL.

By Hoakie, he must have seen a Ghost,
For soldiers have told me—men of good faith—
That they had often seen old Stonewall Jackson
Walking among these tents, straight as an arrow,
And looking very sad; but his last words were—
"Let's cross over the river and rest in the
   shade,"
So if the grand old Captain comes back now,
He must have changed his mind.

Whistles Dixie.

I'm not afraid of ghosts—no not I.

Whistles.

There's no such thing as ghosts, but what our
   fancies make.   *Whistles.*

I'd rather fight a regiment than meet one.

Whistles.

What a clould is rising—is it rain?

Rain begins to fall.

Rain, rain by Jubiter! It hides the moon.
O, I'm not afraid—moonlight or dark.
Whoo—oo—oo—goes there?   Halt! halt!
But, b—b—bt, what's the pass word?

VOICE.

"By the waters of Babylon."

SENTINEL.

Well, that'll do—come in out of the rain—
But you are d—d slow a getting it up.

Enter General Lee.

What, General Lee? Why, General, I catch my
  breath,
A moment more and you as Stonewall Jackson,
Would have fallen by your own soldier.

GEN. LEE.

Had it been so; perhaps it were as well.

SENTINEL.

What, General; no bad news I trust!

GEN. LEE.

No; but I have walked about the camp all night,
And watched my tentless soldiers on the ground;
All worn and weary with incessant fight,
Tho' born to luxury, in beds of down;
Time hastens on, and with to-morrow's sun,
The last battle shall be lost or won.
Keep to your watch—be ready for the fight,
Perhaps we'll meet no more—good night! good
  night!   *Exit.*
SCENE VI.—*Wood—Thunder and Lightning—
  Near Mt. Vernon—Enter Payne—Storms and
  Lightning.*

PAYNE.

No road—no path—no light but the storms
  lightning.
Alas! how many, nursed in downy beds,
In palaces and princely homes, now cry
"No road—no path—no light but the storms
  lightning!"
No voice to cheer them, and no taper's ray,
With long and level beams, from home,

How many a boy, with down upon his cheek,
Stands sentinel to-night, and braves this storm!
Would God that I could lay me down;
But I cannot—dare not—even now
This war of Heaven may beat upon her head.
Mt. Vernon must be hereabout.   Halloo! halloo!
  Enter Beall's Ghost—Payne Drawing his Sword.
GHOST.
Make haste to follow; for my time is short—
One hour remains for me to walk this earth,
And then the fires of yonder coiled Heaven,
Shall spit upon me, with their sulphurous *storms*,
Till boyhood's follies, and my grosser sins
Shall all be purged away—one hour remains,
Then follow thou—till this Confederate grey
Dissolves in morning light.
                                    Exeunt.

SCENE VII.—*They go around the scenes—Mt.
  Vernon opens and reveals Lilly scattering flowers
  and singing—Storm passed and moon going
  down—Tableaux to suit the song.*
          LILLY BEALL, *singing.*
                I.
Now an angel flies, from the field of blood
All glorious to yonder mound—
Mount Vernon groans—'tis the great and the
    good—
Old Virginia's heroes around—
Lee's father sheds a tear, while he smiles on his
    son,
And Stonewall is kneeling by a moss-covered
    gun,
And Freedom lies pale on the ground.
                II.
You moon sinks down over land and wave,
And the fallen lie cold her beams—

Not a funeral gun—no honors for the brave;
But each brow with glory gleams—
Nor the hooting of the owl over yonder hill,
Nor the melancholy song of the Whip-poor-will,
Can disturb their glorious dreams.
Whip-poor-will, when sinks the day—
Whip-poor-will, in your twilight grey,
Whip-poor-will, when the hermits pray,
We'll pray for the souls far away!

Enter Ghost and Powel.

LILLY.

O, my pretty boy, come home! come home!
And you, my pretty Powel, come home! come
    home!

As they approach, she illudes them, scattering flowers before them.

Exeunt.

SCENE VII.—*Madame Surratt's House—Parlor
—Enter John Brown and Dr. Mary, and Hide
Under Curtains—Booth Standing by a Window.*

BOOTH.

Standing at window.

'Tis now the gloaming hour, and all abroad,
Spirits of darkness, beetle on the air,
Some to gay follies, lead the thoughtless crowd,
And some go dancing down to dens of shame,
While other devils, older than the flood,
Sail out to dip their bat-like wings in blood.
Avant, ye devils! leave me all alone—
With whom? Myself! a murderer! God forbid!
More than ten thousand times have I relented,
And making up this cast, would fain have spared
That poor buffoon—worthiest of all his Cabinet;
For, like the thistle flower, true goodness wears,
A regiment of spears, to cry, "hold off;"
And but for this I would have slain him thrice.

"If it were done, when 'tis done, then 'twere well
"It were done quickly; if the assassination
"Could trammel up the consequence, and catch,
"With his surcease, success--besides, this Duncan
"Hath borne his faculties so meek, hath been
"So clear in his great office, that his virtues
"Will plead like angels, trumpet-tongued, 'gainst
"The deep damnation of his taking off;
"And pity, like a naked, new-born babe,
"Striding the blast, or Heaven's cherubim, horsed
"Upon the sightless couriers of the air,
Shall blow the horrid deed in every eye."

                              Enter John Brown's ghost.

                    JOHN BROWN.

Beware!   Beware!
Aye, had I but sworn as you have sworn,
Nor Heaven, nor earth, nor Hell could hold me
        back,
Nor fright me from my purpose.
Had I but sworn to do't,
I'd pluck my grey-haired sire from the gate of
        Heaven,
And drag him thro' the sulphurous fumes of
        Hell—
Choaking with brimstone fire-brands the voice
That whilome called me son—still beating down
His withered hands, lest Heaven should heed his
        prayer.
You swore to me, amidst the lightning's glare,
And Hell's deep cavern echoed back your vow!
That bargain, for your soul, was clinched in Hell;
And all the powers of Heaven did ratify—
My will, now thine, my bidding thou shalt do;
Then go; prepare thee for thy sulphurous bed.
Put shards upon thee, like the beetle's mail;

Harden thy soul wi' crime; smear't wi' blood,
And so prepare thee for thy home of fire!

Exit.

BOOTH.

Poor, helpless mortals we!   Once sunk to crime,
Down do we fall, with devils, in their slime,
And then grow palsied—helpless for all time!
What, tho' we struggle back and cry "be-gone!"
They whisper to our souls, "march on, "march
  on!"

*Enter John Surratt, high-top boots, and spat-
tered with mud, riding whip, and in rollicking
mood.*

BOOTH.

Welcome, Surratt—most welcome at this hour,
For I need your strong arm and desperate will.

SURRATT.

Well, Booth, I've found the very place to cage
  him—
Fit for a President, and secret as the grave.

BOOTH.

Well, what of it?   Where?   What then?

SURRATT.

Th' old Vanness Mansion, on the river-bank.
South of the White House, garnished for the
  bird.
Its deep wine cellars make a lovely cage,
And three strong men could drag him to its
  doors.
Once being captured, we could hold him there
'Til Mosby and his men came up the river bank.
O, th' old gorilla, ha! ha! ha! what a splendid
  specimen, ha! ha! ha!
How he himself would laugh at such a joke!
'Twould be a funny anecdote for him to tell
Jeff. Davis when we get to Richmond—ha! ha! ha!

BOOTH.

What if we put him in a cellar six feet long!
A coffin for his cage, and worms for company!

SURRATT.

Great God! you're talking like a mad-man,
    Heavens!
Lincoln is not a bad man, though led by dema-
    gogues,
For he means well, and has a good, kind heart.

BOOTH.

Those pur-blind sisters, trundling at their wheel,
Have put the scissors to his naval chord;
You, too, must help them turn, for being in,
And now suspected, how could you escape?
Go, throw away your catechism, boy.
Come, take to tragedy, and be a man.
There's something grand and beautiful in
    tragedy.
Think of it, John—just think—Good Friday,
    John;
Earth's greatest tragedy was acted on this day,
And the whole world repeats it to the sun,
On myriad altars rising to salute him!
O, glorious tragedy, that cannot end,
'Til Heaven's lightnings set the stage on fire;
Angels, and patriarchs, and saints for auditors,
And the Lamb slain, stands up amid the falling
    stars,
King of all Kings, and brighter than the sun.
O, that I, too, could act in such a play!

SURRATT.

In that play must we all act.

BOOTH.

Why, John, to kill a common man—a thing—
A President—that's a mere episode!
Go throw away your catechism, boy!

SURRATT.

I love the South ; but love still more
The catechism which my mother taught me;
Nor less on this day—saddest of all days!
True, I would take him prisoner of war ;
But further, not a step will follow you.
Release me then, and let me fly to Canada,
Not to betray you, for I scorn a traitor,
But t'escape your toils, and save my life!

BOOTH.

You prattle like a child—come, be a man ;
Give up your faith and strike for liberty.

SURRATT.

My faith? Ah, little do you understand it!
That unpretending, simple, childlike faith!
It scatters blossoms even upon the grave,
And robes the very air with immortality!
Bad as I am, and foolish in my weaknesses,
To do ten thousand things, when suddenly
    assailed,
Which faith reproves, and memory weeps upon.
Yet, wilfully I would not yield one precept
Of the grand old faith my mother taught me,
For yon Confederate States and all the world
    besides!

·   *Exit.*

BOOTH.

There's a divinity in that boy's dream,
Which boastful reasons cannot emulate—
Inscrutible, mysterious, divine!
More splendid than the rainbow—tempest born ;
Born of the sun, begot in falling tears—
In tears that fell about the Gate of Paradise—
On Calvary—alas! wherever man sojourns!
The rainbow, but a symbol of that dream,
For aught I know, the shadow of that faith.

9

O, that I could fling these knotted serpents
Up to the stars, or down to Hell!
Could I but see their fiery flakes
All trailing down the sky,
Then would I run to Calvary and cling
To God; but that is past, and all is lost! lost! lost!

Window curtains drop and conceal him—John Brown's ghost crosses the stage.

JOHN BROWN.

Poor, struggling insect, now we part!
My web is woven round your heart;
My work well done, to Hell begone!
And tell them there John Brown is marching on.

Exit.

Enter Herold and Atzerot.

HEROLD.

Come, Atzerot, tell me, what do
You think of this whole business?

ATZEROT.

Vel, if de sheutlemens will pay de
Monish, I can cut de wires, and den
Dey can all runs away.

HEROLD.

But what if they should kill the whole
Cabinet, would that save the South?

ATZEROT.

Ef dey kills one, dot makes no good;
But if dey kills all, den I say ya,
For mit de killin', Europe stop de war, and
De South go free—dot's it, dot's it, my baby!

Slapping him on the shoulder—ha! ha! ha!

HEROLD.

I could undertand it better if Booth would
talk to us, and explain it. Sometimes I think he
must be crazy. Damn'd I do anything but hold
his horse at the theater. He intends, I think, to

kill them all in the midst of the play; for this
evening, at Spotswood's Hotel, he sent a note up
to Johnson, and directly after told me to stand
in the rear of the theater, at nine o'clock, to hold
his horse. I asked him a question, and he left
me gaping like a fool.

ATZEROT.

Seward never goes to theater.

HEROLD.

Then who kills him?

ATZEROT.

Vy, Payne, dot big vellow from de South;
He kill Seward, den, you see, I cuts all de wires
    mit de telegraph.

HEROLD.

Cut the wires? Why, you were to kill Johnson.

ATZEROT.

O, ya, ya!

Enter Payne.

PAYNE.

What of Booth? He promised to be here.

HEROLD.

Don't you think him crazy? What good
Would come of it, even if his plans succeeded?

PAYNE.

He has assurances from Canada—
From men well-posted in the current of events;
That intervention soon would follow,
And the South be saved. His vengeance,
    too,
With mine, cries out for blood. Our ruined
    homes,
Our native land, and every sacred memory
Shout to the patriot soul, "revenge! revenge!"

HEROLD.

How could we justify such wholesale slaughter?

PAYNE.

By precedent. Full thirty Kings in France;
In Germany, a score; and in Great Britain, ten;
Th' assassin's dagger punched down to Hell—
From Brutus, of th' olden time, when Tarquin,
Reeking with Lucretia's shame, fell head-long;
To the younger Brutus, red with Cæsar's blood,
From him to beastly Heliogabalous:
And all those Emperors, slain amidst their pleas-
     ures,
Such was the last resort of Freedom.
O'er-topping insolence, and hired minions drive
The people to despair, then lightning leaps
Upon the patriot's blade, and tyrants fall.

                                        Enter Booth.

BOOTH.

They call this day Good Friday. Good! Most
     excellent!
Beware of treachery—beware! for soon
The Judas of our tribes may hear from me,
That curse of Richard—hear it now:
"When I was mortal—"mine anointed body
"By you was punched full of deadly holes;
"Think on that hour, and me, despair, and die."
Should one arm falter or one heart fail,
Not one of us would live to tell the tale!

                                        Exit.

HEROLD.

Now, what does all that mean? Don't
You see that the man's crazy?
                    PAYNE.
By no means.
Warns you and Atzerot—suspects your courage,
Knowing full well, that should our venture fail,
Through craft or cowardice, or treachery,
The South must then be lost forever.

                                        Enter Lilly.

LILLY.

Ah, ha! I thought to find you here,
And jumped over the moon from yon asylum.
All the stars ran after me and cried,
"Come back, sweet Lilly, come and marry us!"
"No, no, quoth I," first come and fight
With Sizera, and slay mine enemies,
Then will I wed the stars, and all
Our children pretty little stars and flowers!
Stay stay, I'll sing to Stonewall Jackson.
There, there he goes!—poor Stonewall Jackson!
Yon moon sinks down over Stonewall's grave,
And the soldiers are sleeping around;
No tents are spread, no cover for the brave,
But they sleep on freedom's ground.
Nor the hooting of the owl over yonder hill,
Nor the melancholy song of the whippoorwill,
Can disturb their slumbers sound;

Spoken.

But Lee could wake them, and his voice
Was like a trumpet on the morning air.

Sings.

Rise, rise brave boys once more for the fight,
'Tis the last to be lost or won.
Then arm, brave boys, by the dawning of the
      light,
And charge to the foeman's gun!
Tho' few, and bleeding now, we must win for
      the right,
Or sleep upon the field with Stonewall to-night—
'Tis the last to be lost or won.
Once more; brave boys! tho' the shot fall fast,
And your comrades are lying low—
Hark! Hark! yon shout, and the trumpet blast,
'Tis Stonewall charging below.
He charges up the hill! See! see how they run!

He mounts upon the fort and captures every
    gun—
And now he turns them on the foe!
Once more, brave boys, and the battle shall be
    won,
Tho' the millions are pressing around;
Lo, Grant comes up at the setting of the sun,
And a thousand thunders resound.
Ah! few and bleeding now—'tis done—'tis
    done!
The banner of the brave, goes down with the
    sun,
And trails at last on the ground!

                  Enter nurses from Asylum.

O, ye are my brave keepers. I am glad to see ye.
Have you come to my wedding with the stars?

              DR. NICHOLS.

Yes, Lilly, the stars are all in wating.
Come, we must go without delay.

                LILLY.

But will they fight with Sizera, to slay mine
    enemies?
And you, my Payne, my pretty Payne, will you
    fight too?

             DR. NICHOLS.

Yes; all will fight—are waiting for the war.
Come let us hence—haste! haste!

                They drag her out.
              Payne in agony of grief.

              HEROLD.

By Heavens, she was a splendid girl!
But having placed her in th' Asylum.
You have done the best you could—nay, all
That could be done. Come, cheer up Payne,
Be a man. I know its a hard case, cheer up!

              Slaps him on shoulder.

O, that the lagging hours would fly,
And bring me to the tyrant's bed,
To make another Robespere, broken jawed,
And cursing as he plunges into Hell!
His curses inarticulate—himself a hell!
His guilty heart, the hell of hells!

Enter Booth.

BOOTH.

Come, let's be going.   Each one to his post,
In this great drama, to be played with Tyrants;
For when they fall, a universal strife,
Like nature fighting in the womb of Time,
Shall heave volcanoes from a fiery sea,
To blast us all, or make our country free!

Exeunt.

Dr. Mary skipping after them.

DR. MARY.

Ah, ha! I'll have his head, his heart, ha! ha!

Exit.

ACT V.

SCENE I.—*Street—Dr. Mary, Conger and Baker under Lamp Post, in Dumb Show—3 Conspirators pass them.*

BAKER.

Which one's Payne?

DR. MARY.

That desperate looking devil, with a slouched hat.

BAKER.

And that one?

DR. MARY.

That's Atzerot.

BAKER.

And that one?

DR. MARY.

His name is Herold.

CONGER.

Did you not say that Booth was with them?
Your tale don't hang together.

DR. MARY.

Hang together or not, I tell you truly;
As I have often urged before, these men
Are bent on mischief; and this very night
You'll find that I have told the truth.
Come, we have no time to lose.

Exeunt.

SCENE II.—*President's Mansion—President Alone—Room Darkened.*

PRESIDENT.

We promised to attend the play to-night,

But this is *Good Friday.* Heavens! it looks
    badly;
A comedy to celebrate the Crucifixion!
Christ to be mocked and spit upon once more—
Buffoons to buffet him! Pontius Pilate,
Washing his hands, and whining, "*I am
    innocent*
Of the blood of this just person!" yet the people,
Eager to swell the pean of our victories,
Propose a grand ovation to the Cabinet;
O, how their brave hands will clap!
No, no, 'twould never do to disappoint them;
But where now are the hands that clapped on
    Calvary?
There was one there, who could not clap his
    hands!
Great God! He made the thunder clap!
           Enter Booth, drawing pistol.

BOOTH.

This is my chance. I find him all alone!
Most kind and humorous, dear, good natured
    man!
Alas! poor Yorick! with his quips and quids,
And merriment, and anecdote. Alas! alas!
Great Ceasar, too, was merciful and kind;
But Casca held his gown, while Butus punched;
For good is, as good doth. What hast thou
    done?
O, perjured wretch—to promise him a pardon!
Yet break that promise on poor Lilly's heart;
Thou lying tongue. Shall I not pluck thee out!
Thou heart of rottenness, to break her heart!
Shall I not pierce thee with requiting steel?
O, brain accursed! Shall I not punch thee thro'?
O, cursed fiend, to blast my land of flowers?

To slay her sons, and drive her daughters to
    depair!
Behold her fallen! Behold her fallen cross—
No longer flashing thro' the battle storm,   .
But flat upon the ground, her form outstretched
Upon it, mocked, despised and spit upon!
O, time most fortunate! most opportune!
To find him all alone—alone with Death!
Revenge and hate come flapping on the air—
Their dragon wings make twilight; and the stage
Is aptly darkened for effect.
                  Aims pistol and then lowers it.
But where my audience? Where th' unborn
    applause?
                  Puts pistol down.
Bah! such a play would fall like vinted wine,
Insipid and without a beaded gallery,
To clap the climax of a bloody gash.
Those other vultures, too, marked out for
    slaughter,
Would all fly away, at the first smell of power.
Oh, no; I'll first arm him, then, forwarned,
He, too, can join the cast with preparation.
              Puts up his pistol and advances.
We'll meet again, at ten o'clock, your Excellence.
The public all expect you—now prepare;
For you must play your part in this great drama.
Ten o'clock, your Excellence! remember ten
    o'clock.

LINCOLN.

Yes, tell them we shall keep our promise ;
But Booth I thought it nine o'clock.

BOOTH.

Aye, nine, and half-past nine; but ten o'clock,
The climax of the play will punch thro' Heaven,
Like some volcano spouting to the sky,

And drawing to it every heart and eye!
Remember: ten o'clock!

LINCOLN.

Yes, I'll remember; we shall all be there.

Exit Booth.

'Twas on this very day, our Saviour died;
And something warns me—psha! presentiments
Are more absurd than dreams; and yet one
    dream
I never had but that some great event
Came fast upon 't. That dream I dreampt last
    night.
A stately ship was sailing 'gainst the wind,
And struck a rock—my wife cried out,
And waking, vowed that she had dreampt the
    same.
Then, going to the window, I beheld
On the heights of Arlington, a shooting star,
Red as the setting sun, and a huge owl,
As tho' some warning hand were laid upon me,
A something strange, that comes to press me
    down—
For ought I know, my mother might return,
To lay once more her hand upon my head;
For well do I remember those sweet hands,
And how they fell, like gentle dews from
    Heaven,
When on her patient lap my prayer was breathed.
This night, for ought I know, may be the last;
And she who loved me then, must love me still.
'Wise fools may ridicule such thoughts,
But mysteries, never yet, by them, explored,
Do rock our cradles first—then dig our graves!
The whence we came! The why we linger here?
And whither? when our spirits take eternal
    flight—

All this, and more than volumes could express,
They know not; neither can they tell why
     dreams,
Like couriers, come upon the midnight air,
To bring us messages, then go their way.
One thing I know, that something makes me sad.
           Rings a bell—Enter Servant.
     Albert bring in the children, Tad and Fred
                 Exit Servant.

This very day some eighteen hundred years ago,
The sun grew dark and graves gave up their dead.
At such a time, I have no heart for comedy;
And yet, our promise must be kept.
           Enter Maj. Lincoln and Tad.
     Come, Taddy; tell me what is Easter day?

             TAD.

Our Saviour rose on Easter day.   O, Papa,
Won't you buy us some Easter eggs?
I'm going to the Capitol that day.
Say, Papa; will you buy us some Easter eggs?

           LINCOLN.

Yes; if you'll tell me why they call this *Good*
     Friday.

             TAD.

Because our Saviour died to-day; but Papa,
Did he die sure 'nough this very day?
But Mr. Beecher says he didn't.

           LINCOLN.

Yes, my son; our Saviour died on Friday.
             Enter Colefax.

  Well, Colefax; they say that Grant has gone

           COLEFAX.

Gone, your Excellence—to Burlington, New
     Jersey.
Quite unexpectedly, for Mrs. Grant.
He begged me to excuse him to your Excellence;

Also to Laura Kean—for he had promised
To be present at her play to-night.

LINCOLN.

I do wish we had not promised.

COLEFAX.

Your are expected with your whole Cabinet—
At least the morning papers have it so,
And the whole city will be on tiptoe
To greet your Excellence.

LINCOLN.

I wish I had not promised them.

Enter Mrs. Lincoln.

MRS. LINCOLN.

Shall we go to the Theatre or not?
Come, Mr. Colefax; cheer him up;
He has the blues.

LINCOLN.

Well, get ready; I'll go.   *Bands playing.*
  *Great shouting without—Lincoln and all go to
the window.*

Lincoln reading a dispatch to the people.
MOBILE, ALA., *April* 14, 1865.

Dick Taylor has surrendered. Our
Soldiers are in good spirits, and the
Rebels have abandoned every hope.

E. R. CANBY.
Great shouting.

LINCOLN.

This was their last army. The South surrenders,
And the Union is restored!

Shouting.

Let us remember to-night, my old Motto:
"*Malice to none, but Charity for all!*"
Come boys, play us Dixie, and then given us
The Star Spangled Banner!

Band Plays.
10

MRS. LINCOLN.

Well, it is nearly our time.

TAD, *to Lincoln*

What does mother mean by "our time?"

LINCOLN.

O, we promised to be there, by nine o'clock—
That's what your mother means, my boy;
But there are times in all our lives,
Of which you children know but little.
Our Saviour said to his Disciples once:
"My hour is come;" and all day long those words
Keep ringing in my ear—'twas on the night
Before Good Friday, and about this hour.
Come, we must go—'tis nearly 9 o'clock.

Exit.

SCENE III.—*Street Near Guard House, Washington—Clock Strikes Ten—Sentinel Pacing.*

SENTINEL.

Halt! Who goes there? *Presents.*

Enter Conger.

CONGER.

Hold! hold!

SENTINEL.

Why, Conger, you should have given the
Pass-word—some other Sentinel might
Have shot you.

CONGER.

I knew it was your watch; besides
The pass-word, has been changed
The last half-hour—for a strange
Rumor is afloat.
Take for your pass-word now, "Conspiracy."
Have you seen Baker?

SENTINEL.

No, not to-night.

CONGER.

Nor Dr. Mary Trotter!

SENTINEL.

No.

CONGER.

He was to meet me here; and she was with him.

SENTINEL.

What was the rumor? and why have they
Changed the pass-word?

CONGER.

O, nothing! nothing; but Baker should
be here. I sent him to the theatre.

SENTINEL.

For what?

CONGER.

Hush! hush! sh!

Drums beating—Shouts in the dsitance.

Hear those clattering horses—how they run!
The drums and shouting—what can all this
     mean?

Enter Baker, running.

I was just in time to be too late.
The President is shot!

CONGER.

Great God! killed?

BAKER.

Killed, and several others with him. I left in
     the
Confusion. It verified the last report.
And all that Dr. Mary told us.

Wilkes Booth entered the President's box; was
met by Major Rathborne, who stabbed him with
his sword, Booth, with a dagger, struck him
down, shot the President, wounded several others
and sprang from the box down to the stage,
waving a bloody knife, and shouting, "*Sic Sem-*

per Tyranis, Virginia is Avenged!" Then something about Lieutenant Beall. But the shrieks of the women drowned his voice. In leaping from the box to the stage he seemed to break his leg, for it gave way every step, and his boot dragged after him.

CONGER.

What course did he take?

BAKER.

I followed close upon his track; saw
Him mount a horse behind the theater.
I fired three times, and must have hit him.

CONGER.

Strike the telegraph; set all the bells to ringing;
Call every man to arms!

Bells ring

Enter Dr. Mary Trotter, breathless.

DR. MARY.

All Hell to pay—I told you so—
Seward is killed—cut all to pieces.

CONGER.

Heavens! was he there, too? Did Booth
Kill both? Was he at the theater?

DR. MARY.

'Twas at his house. A tall man
Cut his way into his chamber—killed
Fred Seward first. I saw the wound,
The dorsal muscle of his belly cut in twain—
A cut across the abdomen. The villain
Knocked down other men, then sprang
On Seward like a tiger, stabbed him
Six times, broke his jawbone with
The but of his pistol, as it failed to
Fire, cut his way out, mounted a
Horse—all quicker than I've been telling
You. They say that Johnson, too, and

several others have been killed—all
Hell let loose!

Cries of fire.

Enter number of police and soldiers.

CONGER.

'Tis a vast conspiracy.   The Rebels are upon us!
They've set the town on fire!
Every man to arms—
Kill every Rebel dog you meet,
Whether at home or in the street!

Exeunt.

SCENE IV.—*Madame Surratt's House—Enter
Conger, Dr. Mary, Soldiers, and Surratt.*

CONGER.

Where is her chamber?

SERVANT.

That, sir.

CONGER.

Knocking.

Open the door.

MADAME SURRATT.

Within.

Who's there?

BAKER.

Open the door—surrender!

Kicks it open.

MADAME SURRATT.

Entering in nightgown.

In the name of Heaven, what can all this mean?
How dare you, man—not man, but brute—how
    dare you
Thus to insult a widow in her bed?

BAKER.

You'll soon have a warmer bed than that.

CONGER.

Hell's too good for the bitch—cut her down!

Enter Annie Surratt.

ANNIE.

O, mother, mother! what can all this mean?

To soldiers.

You mongrels, blackguards! out of this house!
How dare you thus insult my mother?

CONGER.

She's arrested for the murder of Mr. Lincoln.

BOTH.

Annie and mother.

O, Heavens! Heavens!! Heavens!!!

Annie rushes to her arms.

ANNIE.

O, mother! mother, dear! that fatal dream! that
fatal dream!

MADAME SURRATT.

Soft, soft, my child. God's will be done.

Enter soldier.

SOLDIER.

Seward is sinking rapidly. Frederick,
His son, was cut across the belly,
And two men servants wounded mortally.
Here's a description of the murderer.

Giving paper.

CONGER.

Take this, Baker; take a squad of men;
Scour the city; bring him in;
By Heavens, we'll hang them high as Haman.

Exit Baker.

Come, madame, tell the truth;
Reveal the plot, and I'll secure your pardon.

MADAME SURRATT.

I knew no plot that looked to murder—none!

Re-enter Baker with Powel, covered with mud.

BAKER.

We found this fellow knocking at the door;
Alarmed at meeting us, and taken by surprise,

He said that he had come to dig a ditch.

CONGER.

For whom?

BAKER.

For Madame Surratt.

CONGER.

To Madame Surratt.

Do you know this man?

MADAME SURRATT.

No, sir; I know nothing of him whatever;
Never saw the man before. Cheer up, Annie;
God sent these soldiers to protect us.
What a Providence! The ruffian might have
    killed us both.

ANNIE.

Aside.

O, mother, that is Powel!

MADAME SURRATT.

What? Powel?

ANNIE.

Yes, Thornton Powel—Payne.

MADAME SURRATT.

'Pon my word, I do believe it is.

Officers searching him.

CONGER.

Reading a note taken from Payne's pocket.

My dear Captain, we expect you by four o'clock;
Have a message from my son John.
Be sure to come.   M. SURRATT.

DR. MARY.

Do you remember the note from her
To Booth, found on his table? Ah! ha!
You said it was nothing. Now you see.
Th' occipital and genital bones! aha!
I told you they would generate. Ha! ha! ha!

CONGER.

To Madame Surratt

And so you never saw this man before.

MADAME SURRATT.

I did not know him in the dark;
That mud upon his face disguised him more;
'Pon the honor of a lady, I did not know him!

CONGER.

O, I guess not. Come, my pretty cut-throat,
How came your hands so soft?
Indeed, you are a dainty ditcher.

PAYNE.

I am no ditcher—told your bloodhounds,
At the door, that I came to dig a ditch,
And I have dug it for my mortal foes!

CONGER.

What do you know of this woman?
What's your name?

PAYNE.

My name is what my father gave me—
A name well-known in patriotic song—
And you may call it, if so please you, Payne;
For this ordeal is a painful one—
Not for myself, but for this generous lady,
Whose hospitalities I once enjoyed,
And which, by accident, I now abuse.
My horse had thrown me, just across the bridge,
And I returned for shelter to her house;
But more, to get a pass hence to her farm,
On pretext of employment there, to reach our
    lines.

CONGER.

What lines?

PAYNE.

Confederate lines, of course.
    Soldiers advancing with bayonets, threatening.

CONGER.

Hold! hold! Await my orders.

This woman—is she one of your conspirators?

PAYNE.

This lady is a most generous soul,
Thro' whom I hoped to get the pass;
But, as the babe unborn, is she most innocent.

CONGER.

Innocent of what?

PAYNE.

Of what? And do you think to trap me? Fool!
Soldiers about to bayonet him.
Back, villains, if you wish to know what I have
done!

CONGER.

Stand back, soldiers, and await my orders—
He wishes to confess.

PAYNE.

But not from fear of death or hope of pardon,
I scorn alike your menace and your mercy,
To vindfcate this lady, I proclaim,
And hurl it on your pointed bayonets,
That all without her knowledge or connivance,
I slew the dog- -your Seward—in his bed.
Soldiers start at him.

CONGER.

Hold! hold! Let him confess.

PAYNE. ·

'Twas I, and I alone, that gave his blood
To that great ocean, shed from better veins,
Which he had poured upon the ground—
Some men, grown fat wi' power, forget
That they are mortal, and themselves secure,
Send you soldiers, like cattle, to the shambles.
Then if a patriot bares his arm to s'rike,
All eyes wall up to Heaven, and fools shout
murder;

Hell shouts "murder," too, for millions they had
    slain;
But Nemesis hath been abroad to-night!
'Twas I, and I alone, that slew the tyrant.

CONGER.

Having escaped so far beyond the bridge,
Wherefore return to seek this woman's house?

PAYNE.

For her sake, and her's alone, I deign to answer
    you;
Then hear the truth, and learn her innocence.
A Rebel, undisguised, she always gave
Her hospitality to true Confederates.
Well-knowing this, I came to ask employment,
Forsooth, upon her farm, to pass your lines,
Expecting her to get the proper pass.

CONGER.

And would she play into your hands?

PAYNE.

Doubtless to aid a soldier in distress;
But had she been a party to our plot,
Would I, a sane man, have sought her house?
None but an idiot could have ventured so!
Her innocence my own destruction, for I came
To ask employment, as I told you,
Only a pretext to illude your guards;
But that fatality, which seems to follow blood,
Engaged her innocence to trap me thus.

CONGER.

Then wherefore fly, or why disguise your face
    with mud?

PAYNE.

You lie; I never fled; but, as a soldier,
Went to report me at the common rendezvous,
And when your watchful guards had intercepted
    me,

And when my horse, ere I had reached it, fell,
And left me powerless to attain the spot.
Still rejoicing that the tyrants had been slain,
I placed my ear upon the muddy ground
To hear the shrieks of their infernal souls,
Landing in Hell. Then strike me, villains! strike!

Great confusion—Soldiers dash at him—Payne
snatches a sword—Exeunt, fighting.

SCENE IV.—*Mt. Vernon—Moonlight—Enter*
Booth.

BOOTH.

All hail Mt. Vernon. Freedom's holiest shrine!
More than a Mecca thou to Earth's bowed mil-
    lions!
O, sacred mound, and you ye skys that clasp it!
Bend down ye Heavens that kiss my native land,
Blue-domed and beautiful! Once more look
    down
And clasp the ashes of my blasted heart!
O, look upon me with your soft blue eyes,
And judge me kindly. Judge my cruel foes!
As Hanibal who struck for Carthage, but in
    vain!
As Brutus when in vain he struck th' ambitious
    Cæsar!
As Cromwell when he slew the guilty Charles!
As Henry when he roused Virginia's wrath!
So I have struck the Tyrant; and would wake
The land of Washington, to guard his dust!
O, sacred shade of him who trampled on a
    crown,
Offered by sycophants—arise and speak!
If ever spirits, in the dusky shades return,
Or when the torn elements, in fiery combat,
Shake Heaven and Earth—or when devoted
    nations

Do tremble and dissolve—then hear my prayer.
Amidst th' upheaving of these mighty States—
Immortal Washington come forth! come forth!

*Ghosts of Washington and other heroes as in Act
1st, Scene II.*

WASHINGTON.

Infatuated and unhappy man!
Already Abel hath been here to tell the tale.
He brought his wounds for me to bind them up,
And piteously complaining thro' Eternity,
Reveals to trembling ghosts his agonizing grief—
Cut off by your abortive act, he sees
A host of northmen gathering up their strength,
Like Judas bent upon the scent of gold,
To make a war more dire than that surceased!
But for your tragic deed, Abel had brought
A sacrifice of corn and wine and oil
To stay the maddening flood and save your
        country!

BOOTH.

O, useless, useless—worse than useless all my
        work!
Deceived by cowards, and by traitors foiled—
My vast conspiracy now dwindles down,
To one poor victim, while my foes survive!
To take off only one, and he the best—
Could bring no benedictions to my native land;
And yet, had I as many hands as wrongs,   ·
As many hearts, and firm as this one proved,
The whole Cabinet had fallen, at my feet.
While over head the Southern cross had waived
My name immortal, and my country free!

Lincoln's Ghost enters bloody.

Booth hides his face.

LINCOLN.

Your deadly ball, shot through my skull,

Went through the South as well, and pierced
    her heart.
Now driven to despair, she well might covet
This Earthy smell of coffins and of bones,
Which I, shut out from day, and doomed to
    snuff.
Had you but left me still the scented flowers;
Your flowers in the South had bloomed afresh,
Savanahs would have yielded golden fruits—
And fiery blasts return to peaceful songs,
A happy people had rejoiced in Union.
Your statesmen, too, had then returned to
    Washington,
But not for punishment. My motto was—
"*Malice to none; but Charity for all!*"
Then fly unhappy man—fly from yourself—
For vain your flight from them who loved me
    well—
Ten thousand swords are now upon your track;
And like a fiery tempest, sweep the world.
Repent, and be you washed, in Jesus' Blood,
Or soon we'll meet again in sulphurous flames,
To which your cruel deed consigns me—go!—
Go cry for mercy, ere it be too late.
Poor man, I pity you. Aye, and forgive you
    too!

BOOTH.

Alas! poor soul, thy words, like sulphurous
    fires,
Consume the very marrow of my bones,
And burn into my heart—a new-born Hell!
O, pluck it out and cast it on yon tomb,
A vain, but earnest sacrifice to liberty.

              Ghost going.

Stay, stay! and strike me if thou canst.

11

O, stay! thou gory thing, or I will follow thee.
    Ghost motions him back—Booth following.
Thou canst not fright me back—I fear thee not;
Tho' Heaven should thunder "no," and Hell
    gape wide—
St'll would I follow thee. O, world farewell!
Foul deeds will up—we follow them to Hell!
                         Exeunt.

SCENE IV.—*A Road—Enter Conger and Baker
and Soldiers.*

BAKER.

Here let us halt; for though we be upon his
    track,
Our men are weary, and the day far spent.
I doubt if we are on his track at all;
For Herold should be with him; and our guide
Declares this man to be alone.
Perhaps she might mistake some other man.

CONGER.

What, Dr. Mary not know Booth?
'Twas she who put us first upon his track,
Brought us his plans, an hour before th' assas-
    sination,
And ever since has hung upon his flight,
As vultures following on the wounded deer.
She swears she saw him on this very road,
And would have killed him but her gun missed
    fire.

BAKER.

Perhaps her heart missed fire, for once she loved
The villain; and these women change with every
    moon.
Her flood of hate might staunch its bloody
    course,
And even now may lure us from his track.

CONGER.

O, never do you fret—I know 'twas he.
She swears she saw him limping up yon hill,
Pale from exhaustion, and his broken leg
Trailing behind, without a splint to brace it—
Doubtless from pain, he tore the splints away,
A hundred thousand dollars the reward!

BAKER.

Had Mary got it—heavens! the boys
Would now be crazy for her.

CONGER.

Crazy for a bag of bones.

BAKER.

Ten thousand men have scoured the Peninsula—
But if we get him—the money will all be ours.
By heavens, we must have it.   Forward march!

Exeunt.

SCENCE IV.—*Scene in a Barn—Booth and Herold
on the Hay and Fodder with a Lantern.*

BOOTH.

Go back, my faithful boy, to yonder house.
Bring me some water, for I parch with thirst;
My wound keeps up a fever, and my eyes,
Are almost bursting from their sockets.
There, take that money, get some brandy, too,
The people here are kind; but very poor.
Force them to take the change, or leave it at their
    door!

HEROLD.

I know that they are close upon us now.
Can you not go further?

BOOTH.

No, 'tis impossible—I must have rest.
Go quickly and return.

Exit Herold.

You clamorous cock, impatient of the dawn,

Stretches his neck to pip the coming morrow;
So they would have me stand a tip-toe too,
To pip that mightier globe--Eternity!
But I will disappoint them—not as Brutus—
Thief like, breaking into my mother's casket,
 no!
But like the tiger, followed to his den.

     Examines his Carbine.

First let me shoot these loads off, to prepare
Fresh supper for my coming guests.

     Fires and lays it down.

Now sleep my last—best, only friend!
But when I call thee up, to meet them, speak!
And make such argument, in curt replies,
As Randolph would have made their Shermans.
'Twas hereabouts that Patrick Henry's tongue,
Unconscious of its prophesy, proclaimed
The forging of our chains—the clash of arms
Upon the northern wind, and cried indignantly:
"I care not, sirs, what other men may choose,
But give me liberty; or give me death!"
Hark! hark! yon lonely whip-poor-will ad-
 monishes,
That they who live without companionship,
Must die, at last, on some deserted heather,
Forgotten e'en by those who listened to their
 songs.
O, that I had his broad flapping wings for one
 short hour!
I'd waltz my broken leg thro' Southern skies,
And sing to-night a merrier song than his.
Alas! such thoughts comfort not with his song;
For, lifted to the skies, he never sings,
But flat upon the ground, and in the darkness,
As I am now.   For nature's last account
Must soon be audited, and struck against me.

'T hese eyes no more shall gaze on Beauty's mould,
 On the bright sun, nor on my Native land;
 This night shall close them with her sable
     fingers,
In that sleep, which morning cannot drive away.
I know it—feel it—see it as reality—
Aye; hear it, in that monitor, whose voice
Grows audible, as time and passion cease.
The blood hounds could not miss me, if they
     would;
And the next sun shall rise upon my corse.
Let them come on; I will not budge; but fight—
And they shall perish with me.

Enter Herold.
HEROLD.

Can you not go further? I'm sure they'll find us.
A man just passed, who says that they are com-
     ing.

BOOTH.

No, I cannot—my leg hurts worse and worse.
You go, but as for me, it matters not
Whether I die in battle, or on beds of down.

Sleeps—Herold snivles and prays.

SCENE VI.—*Road near Barn—Enter Baker,
     Conger, Dr. Mary and Soldiers*

DR. MARY.

The barn is just out there—look sharp!

CONGER, *to Baker.*

Surround it quickly.

*Exit Baker, with a squad of men.
     Booth's voice in the distance.*

List! list! I know the villain's voice.

BOOTH.

"O, coward conscience, how thou dost afflict
     me!
Give me another horse; bind up my wound."

DR. MARY.

Hush! hush! 'tis Richard, acted in his sleep!
Oft have I heard him thus upon the stage.
'Tis Richard's dream—that horrid dream again
O, can we not spare him?—yes; spare his life!
For he was always generous and brave!

Enter Soldiers.

CONGER.

Forward march!
That way soldiers—double quick.

Going.

Exeunt all but Dr. Mary.

DR. MARY.

Alas! poor woman's heart—its anger flies,
And turns to pity, when the false one dies.

Exit.

SCENE VII. — *Scene in the Barn—Booth and
Herold Sleeping.*

BOOTH.

Take down that banner—take it down, I say!
Once did I love it, but its bloody stripes
Are now like great red gashes in the sky.
"O coward conscience, how dost thou afflict me!
"Give me another horse! bind up my wounds!
"It is now dread midnight—
"The lights burn blue—
"Cold flareful drops stand on my trembling flesh.
"What do I fear? myself! there's none else here.
"Is there a murderer here? No; yes—I am.
"Then fly! What, from myself?
"My conscience hath a thousand several tongues,
"And every tongue brings in a several tale.
"Murder! stern murder in the direst degree!
"Throng to the bar crying—guilty! guilty!

Leaps up

"Have mercy Jesus! Soft, soft; I did but
  dream."
Thank God 'twas all a dream! a fearful dream!
Or, rather, Richard played upon my sleep.
I am no murderer, but the South's red arm
Thrown up in anguish, as her great heart broke!
Then let me perish with my native land,
And as she fell on Patrick Henry's grave,
So let me fall, to mingle with his dust,
Still gasping those immortal words:
"Give me liberty, or give me death!"

    Knocking and voice without.

   VOICE.

Open this door.

  *Booth and Herold listen—Booth examines Car-
bine and pistol and dagger.*

   BOOTH.

I should have loaded it before we slept.

     Loading.

  BAKER, *without.*

Surrender or I'll set the barn on fire.

    Dead silence.

Open this door. Surrender or I'll set the
Barn on fire. Open, I say!

   BOOTH.

Who the devil are you? What do you wish?

   BAKER.

You are my prisoner; fifty men surround you;
There's no chance for escape; be quick; surrender!

  Booth levels his Carbine on Baker.

   BOOTH.

No, I'll spare his life, for that he comes obedient
To the same Tyrant, whose heavy hand I feel.

   BAKER.

Come, surrender instantly—here goes the match;

I'll set the barn on fire,   Will you surrender?

BOOTH, aside.

I have but one load in my carbine yet.
O, for a little time!

Aloud.

This is a hard case Captain: give us a few mo-
    ments
For consultation.   *Loading pistol.*

BAKER.

I'll give you just three minutes.

BOOTH.

That will be sufficient.

HEROLD.

Let us give up; we have no chance!

BOOTH.

And you desert me, too? Go! coward, go!
Captain, a man here wishes to surrender.
    Herold bolts to the door crying and pleading.

BAKER.

Go back, and bring your arms.

HEROLD.

I had none, sir.

BAKER.

Yes, you had, d—n you! You had a carbine!

BOOTH.

On the honor of a gentleman, he had no arms;
They are all mine;
Draw your men off, and fight me one by one!
For I am lame, Captain; give a lame man a
    chance—
Draw off your men but fifty yards.

BAKER.

Your time is almost out.

BOOTH.

Then, my brave boys, prepare a stretcher for me.
But Captain, as you came, I spared your life—

And took my carbine down—give me a chance,
And fight me like a man—fight one by one;
For I am lame, and cannot—would not run!

BAKER.

We did'nt come to fight; but to take a murderer;
The time is out—will you surrender?

BOOTH, *drawing himself with desperation—
Carbine pointed.*
No - damn you! no!

    Barn blazes—Firing on all sides.

BOOTH, *having his Carbine poised, and leaping from side to side, to see them.*

I'll take you down to Hell or up to Heaven;
Cowards! by darkness covered, you are safe;
Fire! for I am in the light, and you in dark-
  ness.
Fire! for I just spared your life—take mine!
Fire! for I am lame and one to fifty—
'Twas thus you fought us from the first,
But from this wave of fire, with plunging shot,
I'll glut the maw of Hell! Infernal fiends!

 *Staggers back mortally wounded—Lincoln's
Ghost rises and supports him.*

LINCOLN.

The South is conquered, and the Union saved—
A mad but generous valor lead them on,
And there was greatness in their fiery zeal.
Put out these flames, and let us all forgive!
My motto from the first hath been:
Malice to none, but charity for all.

 SCENE VIII.—*Street in Washington—Enter
   Citizen.*

1ST CITIZEN.

There they come with Wirtz.

2D CITIZEN.

Hell! there's a rope around his neck.

1ST CITIZEN.

Yes; d—n him; he starved our boys at Ander-
sonville.

*Enter Beau Hickman, a decayed Virginia
gentleman, whose gracious manners always se-
cured him friends and money.*

BEAU HICKMAN.

What's to pay here?   What's going on?

2D CITIZEN.

They are about to hang Wirtz, but
Its a d—n shame to hang him!
And let Lee and Jeff Davis go.

BEAU. HICKMAN.

No one should be hanged, for war means ruin;
And now that war is over, peace means peace—
After such sufferings, I would not harm a fly—
But more than that, three in the North,
For every Captive in the South, have perished!
The North had everything to cherish life;
While the South was ruined and her sons starv-
ing.

1ST CITIZEN.

Martyrs I suppose.   Was Booth a martyr, too?
Shot in a barn and murdered like a dog!

BEAU HICKNAN.

Alas! poor man; I knew him long and well;
And many a favor has he granted me—
Was always kind, when other friends grew cold,
And condescendingly would sometimes play
My subject, in that kingdom of my own,
Which levied contributions on mankind –
A *five* or *ten* or *twenty* he would pay
In lowly reverence to my Majesty.

By Heaven! he played 't so well, I thought my-
    self a king!
Poor Lincoln's blood must ever soil his fame,
But still his dread misfortunes touch my heart—
And gratitude can palliate his crime;
No Christian man could justify the deed—
The fault of madness, rather than his own.
A cold and creeping horror thrills my heart!
And sane, his generous soul had shuddered too;
For he was cast in nature's finest mould—
True to his friendships; for a friend would die;
But scorn'd the faithless, with a burning hate!
With love inordinate, he may have loved
The very mountains of his native land—
Once loved the Union and her rainbow flag—
He loved yon Capitol, his fathers built;
And 'gainst the tempest vainly struggled there;
A shattered rainbow, bending to its dome,
His spirit rose and vanished in the storm!

Enter Policemen.

POLICEMAN.

Stand back! stand back! the funeral is coming.

1ST. CITIZEN.

It' not the funeral, boss; they are only
Moving the President's remains—
He's off for Springfield.

POLICEMAN.

It's all the same—funeral or no funeral—
Clear the streets!

  Enter soldiers, dragging Wirtz, rope around his neck.

Funeral procession.
Exeunt.

SCENE VI.— *President's Mansion — President Johnson and General Mussy Drinking..*

JOHNSON.

What of the murderers?

MUSSY.

They've all been tried and all convicted.

JOHNSON.

What proof against Atzerot.?
What does he say of Madame Surratt?

MUSSY.

That she is innocent.

JOHNSON.

And Herold; what does he say of her?

MUSSY.

Protests her innocence—so do they all;
Yet known to be a Rebel, and so linked
With many enterprises of disloyalty,
No power but your own could save her;
And I implore, your Excellence, to interpose.

JOHNSON.

Why, Mussy, should I pardon her, the mob
Would sweep us all away.
They thirst for blood; their vengeance must be
    slaked;
Let no petition come to me, for God's sake!
Keep the preachers all away, and the women.
But Payne—of course he'll swing.

MUSSY.

True, he's guilty; but his frank confession
And defiant port—his fierce encounter, too,
With Seward's sons, and then his desperate
    fight—
Disputing every inch and courting death,
Excites the sympathy of all our soldiers.
I saw him pass the Market house, in chains—
Like Bryants hero—even more sublime;
"Upon the market-place he stood,
"A man of giant frame;
"Amid the gathering multitude,

"That shrank to hear his name;
"All proud of step and firm of limb;
"His dark eye on the ground,
"And silently they gazed on him,
"As on a lion bound."

JOHNSON.

That reminds me of some po'try I made
When pushing my tailors' goose, in Tennessee:
"If you want the gals to love you,
"If you want 'em to love you true,
"Come down to Andy's tailor shop,
"And git a long-tail blue"—ha! ha! ha!

Enter page.

PAGE.

A lady, please your Excellence, at the door.
She weeps and trembles; wrings her hands, and
     moans
So pittiously we could not keep her back.
Annie Surratt, your Excellence.

JOHNSON.

For God's sake, Mussy, keep them all away.

Exit.
Enter Annie Surratt.

MUSSY.

You cannot see his Excellence.

ANNIE.

O, sir, if you have mercy in your heart;
If e'er you had a mother, and remember
How she loved you more than life itself,
And how, when sickness perilous dire
Had laid her darling at the gate of death,
Forgetful of herself, she lingered there,
Supplied your wants and dried your parchèd
     tongue;
How, by your couch, the livelong night, she
     watched,
And watered, with her briny tears, your pillow,

Oft lifting up her streaming eyes to Heaven,
To bring all Heaven down about her child;
O, then be pitiful—be generous to me—
Implore the President, that I may fall
Upon his very feet, to plead for her,
For my poor mother, O, so sweet and innocent!

MUSSY.   *Aside.*

This ordeal is most terrible.
And I can scarce go through't.
Poor girl! already have I plead in vain.

Sternly.

It is imposible—you cannot see him.

ANNIE.

O, my mother! mother!   *Exit, sobbing.*

SCENE VII.—*At Door of Arsenal—Sentinels
Pacing to and fro—Enter Soldiers and Preacher
with Atzerot—Heavy Chains—Also Herold—
Snivelling and Sobbing.*

ATZEROT.

O, shentlemens! shentlemens!
Take ware! take ware! O, pity me!

1ST. SOLDIER.

I'll preach your funeral—keep a stiff
Upper lip, brother, you'll soon be in
Heaven! All you rascals go up happy!

ATZEROT.

O, mine Got! mine Got! dat is not
Vat I wants—O, mine Got!

*They thrust them in prison door—Thrust Herold
in, sobbing.*

1ST. SOLDIER.

Go now, first to your blindfold warning—then to
        death;
No law's delay—no lawyers with their tricks,
But martial law, to speed the felons' doom!

2D. SOLDIER.

As high as Haman shall they swing,

For all who enter that dark door, leave hope
    behind!

1ST. SOLDIER.

Hammering within.

Hark! hark! Those scaffold-builders hammer
    down
The voice of lawyers and proclaim the law.
O, glorious martial law, that e're it mocks,
The culprit with a trial, builds his jumping-
    board!
All other courts would pull the scaffold down,
Or let it rot between the sluggish terms;
But martial law delights in expedition—ha! ha!
    ha!

2D. SOLDIER.

When did the court convene? Were all tried?

1ST. SOLDIER.

Tried in a horn! ha! ha! A drum-head for the
    judgment seat,
A quick decision, and a winding sheet! ha! ha!
  *Enter Madame Surratt with soldiers—Father
Walters at her side—She bears a crucifix.*

MADAME SURRATT.

O, I do tremble so, yet innocence should give
My poor knees firmness and sustain my heart.
Why, Father, should I tremble like some guilty
    thing?
You know that I am innocent?

FATHER WALTERS.

Yes, child; yes, yes! Be calm, my child!
Our Divine Lord fell beneath his cross!

She Staggers.

  *Father Walters sustains her, and presents the
crucifix—Madame Surratt kisses it.*

MADAME SURRATT.

Yes! Thou can'st strengthen me, for, all alone,

Thy precious feet did climb to Calvary,
Aud three times didst thou fall beneath thy
    cross.
What wonder then, that I should tremble so,
With all my sins to weigh me down!
O, glorious honor, thus to follow Thee!

Enter Annie Surratt, sobbing.
Enter Payne with heavy chains.

ANNIE.

Mother!

*Soldiers holding her back—Weeping and sobbing
of mother and child.*

PAYNE.

God hath no thunder left in Heaven;
And Hell no power to gape her ebon jaws,
Or earth would open wide, for yonder dome,
With all this martial power to topple down,
And save this woman from her doom!!

MADAME SURRATT.

Soft! soft!   There is a judgment yet to come,
And God witholds his thunderbolts 'til then;
Meanwhile, my murderers one by one shall fall,
'Till suicide and misery engulf them all.
May Heaven forgive!   They know not what
    they do.
Farewell, my friends!   To all farewell—
And thou, my child, a last and long farewell!
Heaven's blessings on the child—farewell,
    farewell!

*They thrust her in prison—Push Payne with
bayonets—He sweeps them off with his chains.*

PAYNE.

Stand back, villains!   Let me walk into my
    tomb!   *Curtain falls.*

www.ingramcontent.com/pod-product-compliance
Lightning Source LLC
Chambersburg PA
CBHW021132020726
47500CB00003B/1046